The En

Dedication:

This book is dedicated to my late husband Jackson McBaine(Bear) who died June 10 2004.

I would like to thank my two sons Donald and Stephen Irwin for being supportive of me.

Tanya McBaine Jack's (Bear) daughter.

My two grandsons Isaiah and Nathaniel Irwin whom I love dearly.
My dear friends Shirley Winslow and her son Joe Fields who helped edit and assemble and publish the book.

My friends Janice Gallup, Jean Ballow, my cousin Sharon Hart, my sister in law Pam Deaner, my sister in law Shirley Axe and all the people who believed in me.

I want to give God all the praise and glory for giving me the talent to write. My God reigns. He is an awesome God.

Janet McBaine

The Emerald Ring

Chapter 1: The Silver Bullet...............1
Chapter 2: The Bar-B-Que................22
Chapter 3: The Cabin.......................46
Chapter 4: The Interview..................54
Chapter 5: On the Job......................61
Chapter 6: Gathering The Evidence..80
Chapter 7: Up in Smoke....................85
Chapter 8: The Picnic.....................100
Chapter 9: The Zoo........................106
Chapter 10: The Narrow Escape.....116
Chapter 11: Meeting the Family.....161
Chapter 12: The Wedding Plans......196
Chapter 13: The Wedding..............256

Chapter 1: The Silver Bullet

Sam met him one night at the Silver Bullet when she was out with her friends Donna and Debbie. She had overheard some women talking in the ladies restroom about the man called Bear.

She had to admit he was beginning to spark her curiosity some. All in all trying to get her attention was almost next to impossible. If it wasn't in the same league as a major earthquake or act of Congress you might as well forget it. Sam just wasn't interested in having a man in her life right now.

Sam enjoyed going out with her friends on Friday nights. She liked country dancing. Sam would never refuse a dance with a man if he was a good dancer, unless he was drunk or something and Sam didn't go for that.

I remember once she had asked a man to dance who was in a wheel chair. She thought the man must have loved to dance at one time or he wouldn't keep coming in here week after week. The man braced himself and very slowly she guided him across the floor, braces and all. The man thanked her and she told him that it was her pleasure. He had told her that he was

1

in a car accident and didn't think he would ever get to dance again. She told him to never give up and to keep trying, nothing was impossible, especially with her friend, Jesus. That night she introduced him to her Lord and Savior. Later that night she noticed several other women trying to dance with him and he looked so happy. For him it was a dream come true and you could see a new faith and that hope had entered into his life once again.

Sam liked going to the Silver Bullet because she liked to hear the band "Brandy Station". She loved country music. Let me change that, I don't want to give you the impression that country music was all that Sam liked to listen to. She likes all kinds of music. She just preferred country when she went out dancing.

On her way back to the table she noticed the man that seemed to have captured everyone's attention. She remembered back to one night last week, she recalled seeing him with a lot of women huddled around him. Sam didn't get a very good look at him. She did see him tip his hat and in a polite sort of way said ladies, and walked away.

At that moment Sam was wondering if this man knew how to dance. He had captured her

The Emerald Ring

attention without her realizing it. Most men would have let all that attention go to their heads. I guess that was one of things that impressed Sam the most about him.

It was starting to get kind of stuffy inside the Silver Bullet so Sam found Debbie and Donna and told them that she was going to go outside to get some fresh air. They asked her if she wanted them to go with her and she told them no, that she would be alright.

Outside Sam took a deep breath of fresh air and relaxed for a minute when she noticed the man everyone was talking about, Bear. He was leaning against a tree. He looked like he was deep in thought about something. I wondered what he was so deep in thought about. Little did Sam know that what he was thinking about was her. He was trying to think of a way to get to know her. He knew it wasn't going to be easy. From his observation of her, she only hung around a few people.

Everybody loved Sam. She was just like everybody's big sister. The men of course secretly wanted to be her special fella, but they would take whatever relationship they could get with her.

She noticed that the handsome guy had on

a buckskin jacket, tight blue jeans, western boots and a cowboy hat. his shirt was unbuttoned a quarter of the way down. *Very sexy looking! He had his hair tied back behind his hat. Boy, did he look handsome. Yep, this man definitely has my attention*

For some reason Sam felt compelled to go over and start up a conversation with him. What am I going to say to him when I get over to him? What if he doesn't want to be bothered by anyone right now? Oh well, here goes.

Sam looked up at him and in a shy voice said "Hi there". "How's it going?" He said, "OK", "You been coming here long?" "About a year now." "I like to come here to dance." "It's hard to find a place to go where you don't have to worry about someone hassling you, or causing you a bad time."

"I've met a lot of nice people here and they all seem to watch out for me. They don't know it but I can take care of myself. It's a good feeling knowing that people are watching out for you. When I'm ready to go home they make sure I make it to my car and get home alright." "Do you like it here?" "I like it fine now."

"My name is Bear." "My name is Samantha, but everyone calls me Sam." "Well, guess I'd better get going now." "You have a good time and I guess I'll see you around." As she walked away she could hear him say in a raised voice so as she could hear, "You can count on it."

Well, he's something alright. He's got a smile that would melt your heart away if you didn't know any better. His smile was a real devilish one. The kind that told you right from the start you're in for more than you bargained for. She was thinking that she'd better be careful.

Sam started back in when she ran into Jake. "Jake do you know anything about that man over there?" "his name is Bear". "Why do you want to know Sam?" "Just curious, that's all." "I know that he is three quarter Cherokee Indian, Scotch Irish and an all American. He's fought in two wars and was trained in Special Forces. Quite a combination, huh? I also know that he was not the kind of person you want to get on your bad side. Shamrock told me he saw him mad one time and his eyes turned fire red. His voice was like thunder and he believed that even the pillars in hell shook when he walked. Nope, not someone I'd want to mess with. He pulls 1700 pounds with his legs and lifts 500 pounds with his arms. You need to talk to Shamrock, Bear is his best friend." "He is?", Sam replies. Jake goes on, "yeah, he's known him for years." Ok, thanks a lot Jake."

"Sam! There's something else you might want to know about Bear. He's a good man Sam. He believes in helping people but if they venture off and do something dumb, and does a crime then they have to pay the time. We go fishing together. I know that he lives each day to the fullest like it was his last. He said that way he never had any regrets." Sam replied, "Good thinking." Jake asks "Would you like to meet him? I'll introduce him to you."

"No, that's alright I'll see him around sometime, it's no big deal." "Oh, by the way Sam, he doesn't have a work schedule like everybody else." Sam asks, "Why not? "He's a police detective and he has his own work schedule." Sam said"I see. Sam went back in to find Debbie and Donna back at their table. No sooner had she reached the table when Steve pulled her out on the dance floor. Rest time was over. After a few dances Sam headed for the ladies restroom.

Sam had had a long day and decided to call it a night and go home a little early. Sam went to tell the girls that she was getting ready to go on home. They asked her if she wanted them to walk her to her car and she told them no, she would be ok.

Sam started to walk away when she heard the girls call out to her all excited. "What?" Donna said "Don't look now, but that man Bear everyone is talking about". "Yes" said Sam. Debbie said, "Well, he's coming this way." Sam said "You're kidding!" Debbie says "No." "You can't go home now". Sam asks "Why not?" Debbie said "He's heading for this table." "How do you know Debbie?" Donna told her "We'll find out in a minute. Sam told them that he's probably going to ask one of them to dance. Debbie said,"I don't think so Sam" "I've never seen him ask anyone to dance."

Bear headed straight for Sam. When he got to the table he held out his arm and didn't say a word. He looked at Sam. They gazed into each others' eyes for a moment when Sam suddenly puts her hand on his arm and he escorts her to the dance floor. Everyone stopped to watch. It was like poetry in motion. It was beautiful to watch.

When the dance was over he escorted her back to the table, still not saying a word, he tips his hat, gazes into her eyes, kisses her hand and walks away. Sam was in awe. They kept asking Sam questions but she couldn't answer them. She didn't know what to say. Sam excused herself and said she was going home. "Talk to you later." Sam "Be careful going home". "Ok I will.

On Sam's way out to the car she ran into Shamrock. "Hi Shamrock." How's it going?" "Pretty good Sam.", "How's it with you?" "I can't complain." "That's good." "Shamrock, Jake told me you know Bear." "I sure do Sam. Why?" "Oh, I was just wondering, that's all. Everybody was talking about him and I was just curious. It's not important." "Hey Sam, this is Shamrock you're talking to. What do you want to know Sam?" "I don't know." "Ok Sam, you got a minute." "Sure, I was just heading for my car." "I thought I would go home early tonight."

"I guess you could say that Bear is my best buddy. He's like my brother. Every year we attend the powwow on the reservation. We usually compete in all the competition. Bear has his own 35 foot teepee. We sleep on his bear skin rugs. He killed the two bears himself. He is quite the marksman. There are not too many men that can hold a candle to him. He is in a class all his own. He's considered a marksman in tomahawk, ax, knife, hatchet, guns, (including black powder) and the bow and arrow. He's also good at martial arts and

The Emerald Ring

Indian wrestling." He laughed a little and said "He even had his own canon." "Imagine that." "Anything else you want to know Sam?" "No." I'd better be going home now. That's an awful lot to comprehend being in one person. He sounds like one hell of a guy."

"I'll walk you to your car." "Ok, that would be nice."

They started toward the car, and guess who started heading toward them? You guessed it, it was Bear. "Hi Shamrock." "What's up?" "Hi Bear, I'm just walking Sammy to her car. "Mind if I tag along?" "Sure that's ok. Well, here we are.

They offered to stay until she got her car started. "Thanks guys I really appreciate it!" Just her luck her black 1979 T-Bird with a 402 engine wouldn't start.

Bear offered to try to start it for her but it still wouldn't start. Bear suggested trying to jump it. Sam told them she didn't have any jumper cables with her. Bear said he had some in his truck and he'd go and get them. "Thanks. Bear."

Sam told them she'd get the license number off the car parked in front of her so they could move the car. Bear told her that it wouldn't be necessary for her to do that. Sam said, "Bear you can't jump my car with that car in the way." "I'll take care of it Sam." When Sam turned around she saw Bear picking up her car and shoving it backwards. She could not believe her eyes. Sam just stood there in a trance. Bear got his truck ready. Then he and Shamrock got her car started. Shamrock looked at Sam and asked her, "Are you ok?" Then Bear says, "There you go stuff, anything else I can do for you?" "No, but I really appreciate your help." They replied, "You be careful going home." "I will. I don't live that far from here. See you guys later." Before pulling out, Sam looked out her window and looked up at Bear and said, "Thanks for the dance." Bear tips his hat and says, "Anytime."

Shamrock looks at Bear and says, "I think you made a good impression my friend."" You really think so?" "What do you think?" "I hope so." Shamrock asks Bear, "What's this about a dance?" "I've been trying to find a way to get her attention."

"She did come over and talk to me for a few minutes about an hour or so ago. I saw her go back in and I took a chance and asked her to dance." "It must have been some dance." "Did you say that she came over and talked to you?" "Yea, why?" "My friend, that lady doesn't go out of her way to talk to anyone." "is that right?" "Do you have any idea how many men have been trying to get her attention?" "I can imagine." Bear says, "Just the other night when I saw her walk to the bar to get her Pepsi, every man she passed tried to get her to notice them somehow. She sets her eyes straight ahead, goes to the bar and then straight back to her table. What's more amazing, no matter how drunk the men get, they never give her a hassle. She is one respected lady and everybody loves her."

I'd bet if you talked to each one in here, at one time or another she has gone out of way to help them someway. That's the kind of person she is. I remember one night when I came in here late she had just gotten off the dance floor when about ten men had come in and circled around her. Just as she was about to excuse herself to them, one of the men she usually dances with grabbed her hand and pulled her onto the dance floor. "There is something about her that draws you to her. Bear says "She's a special lady alright."

"I guess since you're so interested in her Bear, it's time for you and I to have a little talk. You see no one in here knows anything about her outside this place." "Why not?" "That's the way she wants it. Sam is a very private individual." "So how come you know so much then?" "It all came about purely by accident. I promised her that I would never tell anyone."

"Sam lives on a horse ranch outside of town. Her grandfather left it to her when he died along with a lot of money. Sam raises horses and has a man run the ranch for her. I guess you might say Sam loves all kinds of animals." "That's good." "Sam also has a special pet named Baby. It's a pet cougar she found one day on the ranch. Something had killed its mother so she took it home and raised it from a baby. It's spoiled rotten and would protect Sam with its life. The cougar is full grown now and has grown into a beautiful cat. Her other baby is a special horse. A blue roam with a star on its forehead. She calls the horse Star. The silverfish color main and tail glistens in the sunlight. Sam is the only one who has been able to ride it."

"Sam's ranch has some of the most beautiful horses you ever laid your eyes on. I also know that she is perfectly content living on the ranch with her critters and the people who run the ranch for her. I think the only time she talks to the foreman is if there is something wrong or if she wants to change something. Bear, this woman is very independent and a very strong willed person."

"Why, I've known her to stand up and fight for things she really believes in and wouldn't back down for anyone or anything whether it had anything to do with her or not. Sam always had a way of getting in the last word."

"I knew her grandfather when he was alive. We would sit and talk for hours. He was a very remarkable man. Sam grew up with her grandfather and I know she really misses him a lot. One day I had gone to the ranch to see if I could go fishing. After explaining to her that her grandfather and I use to go fishing together she said ok, but I was to always let her know first. Sometimes when I go out there she would find me and we would talk about her grandfather for hours. It seems to help her."

"I remember one time when I had gone out there to go fishing, two men had escaped from prison and I just happened to be in their path. The two men had robbed me of my clothes and had started beating me up pretty bad when Sammy showed up." What happened?" She joined in on what she called fun and helped me take charge of the situation again. I don't know what would have happened if she hadn't showed up when she did. We escorted them back to her house and called the police. Bear, I couldn't believe the moves she made on those two men. I don't know where she got her training but this lady is good. I don't think that there is anything or anyone she'd be afraid of. I can still remember her grandfather telling her, "If you have to be afraid to stand up for what you believe in, then there was something wrong and somebody better do something otherwise you might as well lie down and die." Sammy took those words to heart."

"Ever since her grandfather died she takes on every battle she could find. Sam keeps to herself most of the time unless she gets riled about something. Then all hell breaks loose. Sam inherited that trait from her grandfather. Sometimes I don't know if that's good or bad."

"I know of a couple of times she went in to get her gun. She was so mad one day, her grandfather had to take the gun away from her. Sam was on the way out the door as she was loading the gun. Her grandfather grabbed it out of her hands. Sam had tried to explain to him that that man had to be dealt with. He had crossed over the boundaries of even being scum. That he would have to climb out of the gutter just to be considered a low life. Thank goodness the police picked him up and put him away for a long time before Sam could do anything. She finally calmed down after a while."

"Sometimes it's hard to believe Sam takes religion serious. If she hears someone disrespecting the Lord well look out. Sam had a way of preaching to you. She will be having you say Amen before you know it. Believe me; Sam can go on for hours. Before she's finished you'll have tears in your eyes and you will be asking God to forgive you for everything you ever said and done."

"Sam holds the principles of life very high. If you hear of a company treating their employees wrong or doing something not quite kosher, you can bet Sam was checking it out. Once she finds out, she sets a plan in motion and there is no stopping her until it is over and things are the way they should be."

"Sam's foreman's name was Jake and he was telling me one day of her ability to shoot guns. He told me she practices every day but no one has ever heard her shooting or ever been able to catch her shooting. She has all kinds of marksman trophies so she must be practicing somewhere. Jake thought she might have a shooting range somewhere on the ranch but if she does he sure hasn't found it.

Sam is good at martial arts too. I saw that when she helped me that day when I was fishing. Yeah, I think we definitely have to get you two together. Bear I think you might have finally met your match or maybe, even your soul mate."

"Next Thursday I'm suppose to go out to the ranch and look over a horse she has. I mentioned to her one day that I was looking for a horse." "Since I've retired I have more time to ride and can take care of one better now. Sam told me to come on out and take a look at this horse she has. She seems to think it is just what I'm looking for. Why don't you go with me?" Bear said "Sounds like a plan to me."

Bear went home and tried to keep busy until Thursday. Being a detective made it a lot easier. He was in the process of wrapping up a case and had a lot of paper work to do. Time went by swiftly and Thursday morning was there before he knew it.

The sun was rising over the horizon when Shamrock heard a knock at the door. Shamrock knew before he opened the door who it was. You guessed it, it was Bear. "Bear what are you doing here so early?" "Well you didn't tell me what time to be here." "Come on in. Let's get the coffee going." "Coffee?",

exclaimed Bear. "Let's get some chow going."
"Ok" "You get the chow going and I'll go take a
shower and get dressed. After we eat we can
go take a look at that horse." Shamrock got
cleaned up and went back into the kitchen.
Bear had fixed some sausage, eggs, biscuits,
and fried potatoes and gravy. "Bear you sure
do know how to rustle up some grub." After
stuffing themselves they went out to hook up
the horse trailer to the truck. Off they went.
They were there in no time at all. Time seemed
to go by quickly when the two of them got
together. Bear was impressed as they drove
down the entrance to the ranch. They passed
some horses on the way to the house.

"Shamrock, do you think one of the horses
we passed is the one that she has picked out
for you?" "I don't know Bear. I still don't know
how I'm going to pay for the horse. Maybe she
will work out a deal with me on it. All her horses
are top dollar horses. "Wait till you see the
horse before you start worrying about how you
are going to pay for it. You might not even like
it." "I'll like it alright you can bet on that.

Just as they pulled up to the house Sam
rode up on Star. It was quite a sight. Star, a
blue roan with flaxen main and tail and Sam's
dark brown hair blowing in the wind as they

came to a stop. Sam's slim well built body climbed down off Star and headed straight for them.

"Shamrock, you're right, that sure is some horse she has." "Hi Shamrock I see you brought a friend with you." "Yes." "You met him the other night at the Silver Bullet. He helped you start your car." "I do remember. You're name is Bear." "I hope it's ok. He knows a lot about horses and I thought he could help me. Bear loves horses like we do. He used to help his grandfather break horses when he was younger." Sure it's ok this time, but let me know before you bring anyone with you the next time." Sam had Bear and Shamrock follow her to the barn. When they reached the barn Sam picked up the phone and asked Jake to bring the horse out of stall seven to the front of the barn.

While they were both admiring Star, Jake brought a horse around to them named Pacos. "Shamrock, I want you to meet Pacos." Shamrock just stood there for a minute, what a horse. He is thinking to himself that he would never be able to afford such a fine animal. Pacos stood about 16 hands high. A beautiful red sorrel with four white socks and shape of a diamond on his forehead. The mane and tail had been brushed and hung softly as the breeze blew against it.

"Well Shamrock, what do you think?" I love him." " I thought you would." " How does he ride?" "Pacos is a five gaited horse and rides like a champion. Saddle him up and find out for yourself. I'll visit with Bear while you and Pacos get acquainted."

Sam showed Bear some of the other horses while Shamrock rode off with Pacos. Sam said, "I think Shamrock really likes Pacos." Bear says"I do too. I hope he will be able to afford him." Sam said"He will." "I know that is one of the things lying heavy on his mind right now." Sam told Bear that when he gets back, Jake is going to load him up in his horse trailer. He is already loading up his personal belongings. "I don't understand said Bear." "I believe people and horses should be paired up like Star and I are. The horses are a lot happier."

"When Shamrock rode off on Pacos, I saw him take to him right away. He had a certain little prance to his walk and I could tell they were a perfect match." "That's all fine and dandy but paying for him is another thing." Sam said "You still don't understand do you? Pacos is not for sale at any price." "Then why

did you let Shamrock ride off on him?"
"Shamrock is my gift to Pacos. ""Are you
serious?" "Of course I am.. Do you object?"
"No, I think it's great." "Good, now let's go and
get his papers." "Lady, you just made my friend
a very happy man." "Bear you can call me
Sam." "Ok Sam. "

"Do you like to ride?" "Yes I do." Why don't
you come out some morning and we'll go
riding? I'll show you around the ranch." "Ok I'd
like that." "Call me first Bear in case I'm in the
middle of something I can't get away from."
"You got it." Sam asks "What days do you
work?" "Well it all depends." "On what? What
do you do?" "I'm a detective."

"Yeah right." "No really." "Yesterday I just
finished the case I was working on. I'll be
getting a new assignment in a few days."
"Great! If you want, you and Shamrock can
come to a bar-b-que I'm having tonight. It's just
going to be a few of my friends and if you and
Shamrock come that would be great.

"I hope you two come, it will be a nice little
get together." "We'd love to. Look, here comes
Shamrock and Pacos. You're right, just look at
them they do make a perfect match." I told
you." "Well Shamrock what do you think?"
"Well Sam, I sure would like to have him but

he's out of my price range."

"I couldn't believe it. It was like Pacos knew every move I was going to make before I signaled him." While Shamrock was giving Pacos a big hug she asked Jake to go ahead and load him up into the horse trailer. Shamrock yelled, "Wait!" Sam says "You want him don't you?" "Yeah, I sure do." Sam asks, "Then what is the problem?" "I told you Sam I just can't afford him." "Shamrock, Pacos is not for sale." "Then why did you let me ride him and why are you loading him up in my trailer?" "Because Shamrock, you are my gift to Pacos. All I ask is that you take good care of him. You will, won't you?" "You bet I will." "If you ever find that you can't I want you to call me and I will either help you or bring him back to the ranch. Is it a deal?" "Sam you got yourself a deal.

Chapter 2: The Bar-B-Que

"I gotta go now. I have to see the veterinarian before he leaves. He is here for their regular check up. See you guys tonight." While they get into the truck Bear explains to Shamrock that they have been invited out to her ranch for a bar-b-que. "Looks like you're making progress Bear." "I know. She also invited me to go riding with her some morning." "Right on." "Are you going to go?" "You bet!, In a heartbeat. She said she'd show me around the ranch."

"Bear I just can't believe Pacos is mine." "I know, you're a lucky guy alright." "Ok Pacos, you're home." Shamrock pulled up to the barn and Bear opened the coral gate and Pacos went right on in. It was just like he knew this was his home. "Bear, you're going to have to bring up one of your horses now so we can go riding." "Guess so." Bear told Shamrock to have fun with Pacos he had to go. He had a few things he wanted to get done. "I'll see you this evening. I'll pick you up a 5:00. I'll be ready."

You know the saying, meanwhile back at the ranch. Well back at the ranch Sam is getting in frenzy about some corporation called

The Emerald Ring

Janex. Apparently while Sam is having Jim the vet look at her horses he was filling her in on what is going on around the area. He had been called in on a lot of cases of dead animals and fish. He told her how he suspected the Janex Corporation to be behind it. "You know Sam, they're the same company that picks up my hazardous waste. I didn't think at the time to have them checked out to see if they were following the state and federal regulations." "Jim do you know if there is anyone doing anything about this?" "No, I don't think so." "Well, someone should do something about this before it gets any further out of hand." "I agree, but what can we do?" "I don't know but I'll think of something and get back to you." "Well I have a few more calls to make Sam, I'll see you in a couple of months." "I'll call you in a week or so to see if you've come up with anything or not." "OK Jim." "Thanks a lot for coming out." "Anytime. You know that!"

"Mamie, I've got to go into town for awhile. Can I bring you anything?" "No. I'm OK Sam. I don't need anything." "How's everything coming with the Bar-B-Que?" "I have everything organized and it should be ready when your guests arrive. I always know I can count on you." "Whatever would I do without you Mamie? If you need any help, let Frank know and he will help you." Mamie is Sam's housekeeper and has taken care of her since she was a little girl.

On my way to the Courthouse I decided to buy me something. That always seemed to pick me up. At the Courthouse I ran into Tina who owes me a couple of favors. "Hi Tina. How's it going?" "Great! What's up? is there anything I can help you with?" "Maybe" I need to get as much information as I can about a Corporation. I'm checking up on the Janex Corporation. Can you help me?"

"Tell you what. You come back in a couple of days and I'll see what I can do." "Great!" "Thanks a lot Tina. "See you in a couple of days. I really appreciate your help!" "No problem.

Now, to go shopping. *What do I want to buy?* Sam notices a white blouse in the window. It really caught her eye. "

Sam went in to check it out. It looks so feminine and soft. *I don't know, oh well I guess I could try it on. Oh, this feels so soft. I wonder if I would ever wear it though. It is awfully nice. I'm going to get it.* Sam told the lady that she would take it. Mamie will love this. I do feel better, I knew I would. Sam checked in with

The Emerald Ring

Mamie when she returned home to see how things were going.

"Mamie I bought a blouse while I was in town but I don't know, what do you think?" "Oh Sammy, it is beautiful. You can wear it to the bar-b-que. It sure is pretty." "I'll think about it." "You should let people see you dressed up for a change instead of those old blue jeans and boots you wear all the time. Let people see you as something besides a tomboy." "Oh Mamie."

Sam heads out to the barn and works on a few odds and ends she had been putting off. After finishing a few things she heads back into the kitchen. "Hi Mamie, everything ready?" "Sure is Sam."

"Why don't you go up to your room and relax a little bit before the bar-b-que." "I think I will, if you need me for anything I'll be in my room. Ok?"

When Sam reached her room, she reflected back on what Mamie had said about letting people seeing her feminine side. She pulled off her boots and immediately turned on her stereo system. Sam loved soft quiet music when she had a lot to think about. When Sam was alone in her room she was an altogether different woman. It was her escape from the world. Her room spared no expense.

Sam headed for the jet tub and started thinking about what she was going to wear to the bar-b-que. Slowly, she slipped her toes into the water, tickling them, as she submerged; letting the jets massage her body as the steamy bubbles danced across the top of the water, just slightly covering her breasts. Sam relaxes as she watches the fish swim around in a lighted wall fish tank designed for her by an architect. Sam loved to sit and watch the fish while she relaxed in her tub. It was her escape from reality.

Sam got out of her tub and wrapped a soft large bath towel around her as her toes sunk into the plush white carpet and she headed for her bed. Sam went up three steps that lead to her magnificent bed and leaped right in the middle of the fluffy pillows on her bed. Sam laid back and started thinking about the people who were going to be at the bar-b-que. She was always trying to think of ways to get her friend Bobbie and her Uncle Don together. Sam thought they'd make a perfect couple. *I'm glad Shamrock and Bear are coming. That way it won't look so conspicuous to Uncle Don.*

Sam looked up and saw her pet cougar coming. "Hi baby girl, come on up." She taps

The Emerald Ring

the bed signaling it was ok for Baby to jump up on the bed with her. Sam wrestles around on the bed with her and then calms her down and they fall asleep.

Sam sure loves that cougar. Needless to say, Sam had a king size bed. A pet cougar takes up a lot of room. Sam had a pet door installed in the wall separating Baby's' room from hers. A glass wall was built to enclose a special room just for Baby. With a waterfall running down into a stream in the midst of all kinds of flowers and shrubs. It also had special lighting and it is temperature controlled just for her.

Let's see, what do I want to wear tonight? I guess I can wear my black jeans and the new blouse that I bought. The neckline has elastic in it and I can pull it down across my shoulders, maybe. It's hard for me to get into this feminine look. I know I'm a young lady now and I should dress the part at least once in awhile. Ok Mamie, here it goes across my shoulders. This is for you.

I still have little time before my guests start arriving. I'll slip in and set up my computer for the Janex Corporation crack down. Sam codes the computer as Janex 1. *I'd better look and see if I have any books on hazardous waste.*

She looks through her books in her personal library but doesn't seem to find what she is looking for. *I guess I'll have to go to the library in town tomorrow and see if they have anything. I'd better check with Bobbie tonight and see what the legal aspects are on hazardous waste since she is an attorney. Mamie should be calling me any minute now to tell me my guests are arriving. I'd better get dressed.* Sam pushes a button and a mirror slides across the wall concealing the room where her computer equipment and work out area are hidden. The only person who knows about the room is Mamie and her Uncle Don. Her Grandfather had it built in when he had the ranch house built. Sam's hair is dry now so she could brush it out and get ready to go meet her guests. Sam's beautiful dark brown wavy hair would glisten in the moonlight tonight. Sam wore very little make up, just enough to accent her brown eyes. Tonight Bear will be more captivated by her beauty more than ever.

Mamie called her on the intercom to let her know that her first guest Bobbie had arrived. "Thanks Mamie I'll be there in a minute." Mamie fixes Bobbie something to drink and then takes her to the pool area.

"Hi Bobbie." "Hi Sam, what's up?" Have

The Emerald Ring

you heard anything about the Janex
Corporation?" "No, why?" I was talking to my
vet Jim this morning and he was telling me
about the dead fish and animal's people are
finding and bringing to him. Apparently they
have been dying from some sort of poisoning.
He feels that the Janex Corporation might be
behind it somehow. I asked him if he knew if
anyone was doing anything about it and he
said he didn't think so. I told him I would see if
there was anything I could do for him to check
back in with me in a couple of days."

"Do you know of anything that we can do?"
"I'll do some checking for you. Sammy how's
my little girl?" "Hi Uncle Don. I'm sure glad
you're here. You know Bobbie." "Yes, hi
Bobbie." "Hi Don." "You know I wouldn't miss a
chance of seeing my little girl. So tell me what
have you been up to?" "Oh, just riding Star and
puttering around, not really much of anything.
Yeah, since when have you ever not been up
to something? When are you going to come
out and go riding with me?" "How about one
day next week?" "Now back to my question
young lady. What have you been up to?" "Well
Uncle Don I'm really not up to anything yet." "I
knew it; you have your teeth into something.
What is it?" "Have you heard about the dead
fish that keep popping up around the lakes?"

"It's been brought to my attention" says Uncle Don. "I was wondering if you had gotten wind of it yet." "Sam, this is one we might be able to work on together." "All right, says Sam! Let's get together one day next week to plan our strategy."

The door bell rings. It's Shamrock and Bear. Mamie took them to the pool area where Sam and her guests are. "Hi Shamrock, Bear glad you could come." Mamie calls them to start eating. Bear just stands there looking at Sam at how beautiful she looks. Sam smiles at Bear and asks, "Are you ok Bear?" Yeah. When I walked in and saw the way you were standing there with the moon at your back shining through the trees; it just took my breath away. You look so beautiful standing there I just couldn't take my eyes off of you." "Oh Bear, you're very kind. Come on, we better go and eat."

"Everyone eat up, there is plenty of food says Mamie".

Uncle Don sees the interest that Bear is showing Sam and decides to do a twenty questions routine on him. "Bear, what do you do for a living?" "I'm a detective." "Are you working on anything exciting?" "No, as a matter of fact I just closed a case that I'd been

The Emerald Ring

working on the last couple of months this morning." "Great! How long have you known Sam?" "I just met her the other night at the Silver Bullet. Her car wouldn't start and I helped her get it started." "I see", said Uncle Don. "She invited Shamrock out to look at a horse and he wanted me to come with him so I did." "You like horses?" "Yes I do. I have quite a few back in Oklahoma. I have a spread out there." "How big is a spread Bear?" "Oh, I guess it's about 1,500 acres." "Bear, why are you working as a detective here when you have all that?" "I let my Uncle take care of the place for me. He needs something to do and he is good at it. It also allows me to do what I enjoy doing."

"Shamrock and I have been around horses as long as I can remember. I used to break horses for my Grandfather when I was younger." "Sam sure loves, horses", says Uncle Don. "She must. Sam gave a horse named Pacos to Shamrock this morning because she thought it would make the horse happy." "Yeah, that sounds like Sam alright. I just couldn't believe it, is she alright?" Bear said. "Yes." Don said "She's just a little hard to understand sometimes." Pacos is a fine horse,." Don told Bear that he is one of her best. "I could see that. Shamrock is just beside himself. He was telling me that he would like to meet the horse trainer. "Don, do you know who it is?" He told me that he had never seen anything like it. The horse was picking up on everything he wanted the horse to do even before he signaled him to do it. Don said, "Well he won't have to go far." "What's his name? Does he stay here on the ranch?" "The trainer is Sam." "Sam!" "Yeah."She trains all her horses. I don't know how she does it. Those horses will do whatever she wants them to do. Sometimes it seems like they're reading her mind."

"Bear, not to change the subject but have you heard about the dead fish people are finding around here?" "Yes I did. I also heard that there had been some animals reported as well." "Does anyone know what is going on?" "They think that they are dying from some sort of poison. The department keeps getting reports turned in every day about it. I have a feeling that it's going to be my next assignment." "That right?" "I wouldn't be surprised."

"Shamrock I hear you are now the proud owner of Pacos." "I sure am. I just can't believe it. Pacos and I are going to spend a lot of time together." "You have a lot of time to ride?" "I

The Emerald Ring

sure do. I'm a retired truck driver." "That right?" "Yes sir!"

"I hear you knew my brother, Sams' Grandfather." "We used to go fishing together every now and then." "You may not want to go fishing for a while." "Why's that? "Haven't you heard about the dead fish people are finding in the lakes? "No I didn't. Does anyone know why they are dying?" "They think from some sort of poison." "What kind?" "They don't know. Rumor has it the Janex Corporation is behind it. People suspect that the Corporation is dumping hazardous waste in the lakes in the surrounding area." "Then we have to stop them. Is anyone doing anything about it?" "Well, not officially yet. What do you mean?"

"Well Bear thinks that the department is going to give it to him for his next assignment." "I've been asked to look into it unofficially. If I know Sammy she is bending Bobbie's ear about it right now. I guess you could say there are a few people working on it." "If I can be of any help in catching them, let me know." Bobbie and Sam join the guys. "What's up guys?" "Don told them that he had been telling them about the fish problem. "Guess what? Bear thinks that it is going to be his next assignment. Shamrock had offered to help too." Sam says, "Well guys, I think we make a pretty good team. What do you think?" "I think you're right!" said Uncle Don. "Ok, now let's get to work." Bear said, "Sounds like a plan to me. Uncle Don. I have already set up my computer for the job when we need it." "GREAT!"

Bear starts talking to Sam about her computer while Bobbie, Don and Shamrock go and get refills. "Sam, I sure would like to see it sometime, it sounds fascinating." "Really." "Really." "I don't run into many people who know that much about computers. Maybe you could show me a few things I don't know." That's if you don't mind." "Well, you see, it's not that easy." "I'm sorry, I don't want to cause you any problems." "Oh, it's not that. I've never trusted anyone before. The only ones who know the computer exists are Mamie and Uncle Don. All they know is that I have a computer. "

"That sounds mysterious. This is starting to sound complicated. I sure don't want to cause you any trouble." "It's no trouble. We are going to be working together so I guess it will be ok. Bear, you have got to promise me something." "Anything." "What I'm about to show you, you must never tell anyone about." "Ok, I promise. You make this sound like a big dark secret or something." "You might say that. Wait here a minute Bear and I'll be right back."

Sam goes over to Mamie to tell her that she was going to show Bear her computer. "Mamie do you think it will be ok? "He promised not to tell anyone about it." Mamie says, "He promised you didn't he?" "Yes." "Then go ahead, it's about time you started trusting someone for a change." "Mamie, I've only known him for a couple of days." "It doesn't matter how long you know someone. Things like this you just feel down in your gut." "Ok, thanks Mamie."

Sam went back over to where Bear was and said, "Follow me Bear." "Anywhere Sam." "Oh Bear, come on. Bear in a minute all this mystery will clear up and you'll understand my caution."

They go back into the house, through the kitchen and down a long hallway to Sam's room. "I guess I'd better warn you first before you go into my room. I have a pet in there and I don't quite know how she will take to you. "Don't worry Sam I'm good with animals. "Well, you see she is not your ordinary pet." "I see. This must be your pet cougar." "Yes, how did you know?" "Shamrock was telling me about her." "Great! Let's see what happens."

Janet McBaine

Sam opens the door and they walk in. Bear says, "Oh my." "What?" "This room is incredible." "Do you like it?" Sam asks. "This is the most remarkable room I have ever seen, it's beautiful." "Thanks." "Now where is the cougar?" "Her name is Baby and she will be here in a minute."

They walk into the room a little further and Bear sees the room that was built on for the cougar. "Sam, this is absolutely amazing." Sam told him about how her Grandfather had it built when she found the baby cougar and brought it home. "The wall had a pet door in it so she can come and go when I'm in the room. She usually comes in when she hears my door open. "

"Where is the computer? I don't see it." "Come over here." Sam pushes a hidden button on the wall. The mirror starts sliding over until a hidden room appears." It's in here." says Sam. Bear walks in and says "It's awesome Sam, just like you."

They entered the hidden room and Bear is overwhelmed at what he sees. The first thing he notices is the section where she works out. There is a refrigerator and snack bar. Bear says, "So this is how you keep in such fine shape." "Thanks Bear, I work out in here every day. I have a special routine I do." He sees a door and asks, "Is that where your computer is kept?" "No, follow me." Sam takes him over to where she has her computer set up." Wow, This is quite a set up. Not many offices are set up this good."

They sat down and Sam showed Bear how to pull up things on the computer that pertain to the Janex Corporation. She showed him her fax machine and how she can fax things from other offices to her room. She showed him how to use the phone to send things to her computer. Sam also showed him how to down load information to her computer there at home. "Sam, I understand why you don't want anyone to know about this room but I promise I won't tell anyone about this room. You have my word on it. "Thanks Bear. I feel I can trust you, I don't understand why; it's just a gut feeling I have." "You can trust me Sam."

In the meantime Bobbie had gone on home. Uncle Don had given Shamrock a ride home so Bear could stay longer and not have to worry about him. He knew Bear wanted to spend some time with Sam. Mamie was so happy to finally see her interested in someone. Mamie used the intercom to tell Sam and Bear that the rest of her guests had gone home and to let Bear know that Shamrock had hitched a ride with Uncle Don. "Thanks Mamie.

On the way out they go past the closed door again and Bear is curious about what was behind it. "Ok, you want to know what is behind it don't you? Go ahead, open it up." When the door opens a light comes on and he's looking at one of the most advanced target shooting ranges he had ever seen. "Would you like to try it out?" "Could I?" "Sure, go ahead." "Doesn't it make a lot of noise and bother people in the house?" "Look closer." This room is lined with lead, its sound proof." Bear tries it out. "Sam this is great." Sam is impressed with Bears shooting. "Bear you're a good shot." "Thanks Sam. Sam you have quite a collection of weapons here. Can you shoot all of them?" "Most of them, my Grandfather left them to me when he died. We use to practice together. Would you like to come out here and practice? Would I!"

After target shooting they went back into Sam's bedroom where Baby was waiting for them. Sam walked over to her, "Hi baby girl. Bear walked over to her slowly and she took to him right away. "I guess you do have a way with animals. Usually she won't let anyone near me let alone pet her." Bear said "That

The Emerald Ring

right? She sure is a fine looking animal Sam.
You have done a fine job raising her." "Thanks."
Sam and Bear returned to the pool area.
Mamie offered Bear a piece of homemade
apple pie. "Mamie this is very good. I think I'll
take you home with me." "No, I have to stay
here and take care of Sam but you can come
out here anytime you like. Sam if you don't
need me I think I am going to bed now, ok?"
"Sure Mamie you go ahead and thanks for all
your help today." Sam gives her a big hug and
Mamie leaves. "I guess I'd better get going
now", said Bear. I really don't want to go but it
is getting late and I want you to invite me back
sometime and not just for target shooting." "Do
you think that's possible?" "Bear I think that's
very possible. "Thank you for coming tonight, I
really enjoyed your company." Sam walked
Bear over to his truck parked over by the
stables. Bear suggests that they get together
one day next week to see if either one of them
had come up with anything on the Janex
Corporation. Sam agrees and told Bear to call
her and check on a time that would be good for
both of them. Bear starts to open up the truck
door and pauses for a minute, then turns
around and looks at Sam. All of a sudden they
are caught up in a trance looking at each other.
Sam gets a feeling all over her that she had

never gotten before. A few minutes later Bear takes Sam into his arms and kisses her very passionately. "Sam you're a beautiful woman." Bear gets into his truck and drives away before Sam could say anything.

Sam heads back into the house. Mamie asks Sam, Did everything go ok?" "Everything is wonderful Mamie. Mamie smiles. We're all going to get together and work on the Janex Corporation. Maybe as a team we'll be able to clean up the mess they've created." "I hope so Sam." "I'm pretty sure if anybody can get to the bottom of it, we will." "Will bear be coming out here again soon?" Yeah, why? "We're going to get together sometime next week." "Oh, I just wondered if he was. I was going to bake another pie, he's a good eater." "Oh Mamie, you're a sweetheart. I think he'd really enjoy eating another one of your pies."

"Mamie." Yes Sam." "I need to ask you something." "Ok." "Well something happened tonight that I quite don't understand." "What happened Sam?" "Well, I've seen Bear a couple of times before tonight." "Yes." "I was even talking to him for awhile before he left and everything seemed ok. Tonight when he got ready to leave, he started to open up the door to his truck, then suddenly turned around and looked into my eyes for a few minutes. It was like we were in some sort of trance, then he kissed me and told me that I was a beautiful woman, got into his truck and drove off." "He did?" "Yeah. What do you make of it?" "Well I don't know Sam. The question is how do you feel about it?" "I don't know. It has been a long time since I let anyone get that close to me. He complimented me several times during the evening but I hadn't expected him to do that. Why didn't that happen before when I was talking to him?" "I don't have any answers for you Sam; sometimes it just happens that way."

"Mamie it was like we were frozen and couldn't move, but at the same time I felt warm all over and chilled at the same time." "You are one of the lucky ones Sam, most people don't get to experience that moment. What's even sadder, some people don't do anything about it. They pretend that it never happened for whatever reason and end up losing the most valuable gift to man." "What do I do now?" "Just take each day as it comes and it will take care of itself." "Thanks Mamie, I sure do love you." "I love you too Sam." Good night Mamie." "Good night Sam."

The phone rings and it is Uncle Don. "What's up Uncle Don?" "I was reading the newspaper and just came across this Ad I thought you might be interested in it. The Janex Corporation is looking for someone with computer experience." "You're kidding. This is going to be a lot easier than we thought. We will be able to get in on the inside and get what we're looking for a lot faster. With me on the inside it will be a piece of cake." "That's what I thought you would say Sam. This could be dangerous Sam, you be careful." "I will Uncle Don. I'll be there first thing Monday morning with my resume in hand. Thanks Uncle Don, talk to you later." "Good night Sam."

After talking to Uncle Don Sam got ready for bed and went to sleep but she woke up early. She laid there until the sun peaked over Baby's room. The water glistened as it dances across the rocks into the stream. *It sure is a beautiful picture to wake up to. This is my favorite time of day with fragrances bursting in the air and the little wild life scampering all around.*

Sam gets up and heads for the kitchen to get her a cup of tea. Sam likes to drink her tea by the pool where she had a fenced in wildlife area. It contains all kinds of wild life and birds. Mamie brings Sam her breakfast. "Morning Sam. How are you this morning? Did you get

The Emerald Ring

any sleep last night?" "I was a little restless, but I did get some rest. It sure is a beautiful morning Mamie." "What are your plans today Sam?" "I'm not sure yet Mamie. I thought I would work out a little. Do a little target shooting and then take Star for a ride." "You let me know when you get ready to go riding." "Ok Mamie." "Talk to you later."

Sam finishes her breakfast then goes into her bedroom and straight to her work out room and starts her daily martial arts exercises.

After about an hour of working out and a little target shooting to keep in practice she heads for the shower to get ready for the day. Sam got dressed and told Mamie she was headed for the stable to get Star to go riding. Mamie told Sam to be careful. Sam saddles up Star and off they go. Sam sees Jake on her way out of the stable and asks her if she was going to be gone long. "I'll probably be gone all morning Jake. I want to spend some time with Star because I'm going to be pretty busy the next couple of weeks."

Sam and Star headed up to the lake to look around and make sure everything was ok. The lake was so beautiful in the morning and Sam had a favorite view there that was absolutely breathtaking. "I sure would hate to see this place contaminated Star." Star shakes his head up and down as if to agree. "We spent a lot of time up here with Grandfather. This was a special place for us and I dare anyone to mess with it." Sam didn't find anything out of the ordinary so she headed back to the ranch.

When Sam got back to the ranch she rode Star over to the stable. Sam noticed Jake talking to someone when she rode up. She unsaddled Star. After she brushed him down she headed for the house. "Hi Jake. Who was that you were talking to when I rode up a while ago?" "That was your Uncle Don. He was up at the house." "I didn't recognize him from the stable." "He wanted to go riding with you this morning but I told him that you had already gone riding up to the lake." "Thanks Jake."

"Hi Mamie, I'm back." "Hi Sam. Your Uncle Don is out at the pool waiting for you. I fixed him some lunch while he was waiting. Can I fix you something?" "Sure Mamie, that would be great, I'm famished." Sam went to her room to freshened up. Then she joined Uncle Don out by the pool. Mamie fixed her a couple of cheeseburgers, french fries and a big glass of cold milk. "Here you go Sam. How's this?" "Perfect Mamie. You always know just what I need. What's up Uncle Don?" "Sam, I told you

The Emerald Ring

that I was going to come out and go riding with you one day this week." "I know but I didn't think it was going to be this soon. I wish you would have called me this morning and let me know. I would have waited for you." "That's ok Sam. We can go riding another time."

"So tell me, did you enjoy your ride?" "Oh yes. No matter how many times I go up there, it's still just like the first time. I checked everything out while I was up there and I didn't notice anything out of the ordinary." "Well, if there was anything going on there you would know it. You know that place like the back of your hand. You got that right Uncle Don."

Chapter 3: The Cabin

"I've got an idea. Since you're here why don't we go up to Canyon Lake and look around. We can go fishing while we are there. A friend of mine has a cabin up there and told me I could use it anytime I wanted to. We can spend the night there and head back in the morning." "That sounds great Sam." "I will have Mamie pack us up a lunch in case we don't catch anything we will still have something to eat." "Good thinking Sam." "Uncle Don, would you go and get the jeep out of the garage? I'll meet you back in the kitchen." "RIGHT!" "Mamie Uncle Don and I are going up to Canyon Lake and while we are there looking around we thought we would get some fishing in. We will be back sometime in the morning." "I'm glad you and your Uncle Don are finally going to be able to spend some time together. I know he really misses your Grandfather. You are so much like him; it will be good for the both of you. There you go, it's all ready." Uncle Don came in and asked, "Are you ready to go?" Mamie says, "You guys be careful and Don, you take good care of Sam. Don't let anything happen to her." "Mamie you know I wouldn't let anything happen to my little girl.

The Emerald Ring

"Uncle Don I'm not your little girl and I can take care of myself." "We know. Ok let's go." "Give me the keys Uncle Don." "No Sam I'm driving." "Let's flip for it, heads I drive and tails you can drive. Tails." "Oh alright Uncle Don you can drive."

"It's been a long time since we've been able to spend time like this together". "I know I seem to be busy all the time." "I wish I could have spent more time with your Grandfather. I really miss him." "I do too. He talked about you all the time." "He did?" "Yeah, he was really proud of you. You would always hear him say my brother did this and my brother did that. In his eyes you could do no wrong. Uncle Don even though you didn't get to spend much time together, it was like you were always with him. I asked him one day why you didn't come and visit more and he said, "Sam he's always here. He's never more than just a thought away and when I really need him he always show up." "I guess in his eyes you were a hero." "Thanks Sammy." "For what?" "I didn't know how much he loved me until now. Sam anytime you need me I'll always be here for you." "I know Uncle Don."

"Ok, here we are. Let's unpack the jeep. I'll put the food in the refrigerator and if you want to get the fishing gear ready we can go fishing right away." "I'm ready Uncle Don. Whoever catches the biggest fish wins and the loser has to cook dinner." You're on Sammy." Let's set our watches ok? It's 4:30. We can meet back here at 6:30."

Uncle Don goes one way and Sammy goes the other. Sammy's friend Frank had told her where she could catch a good mess of fish so she felt that she was already one up on her Uncle. Uncle Don had found a great spot and started catching fish right away. After catching two big bass, a couple of blue gill and some crappie he notices the time was almost 5:30 and starts heading toward the cabin. Uncle Don just knows that Sammy hadn't got a chance of winning and was feeling pretty good.

On the way back to the cabin Uncle Don notices some men on a raft floating on the lake. *I wonder what they are doing.* Meanwhile Sammy was also heading back to the cabin when she notices some fish floating in the water next to the bank. Sam hurries down to gather them up thinking that they might be able to give them a clue as to what was going on. Quickly she hurries back to the cabin with her catch. Sam's thinking to herself that her Uncle Don doesn't stand a chance of beating her and that he was going to have to fix dinner. Sam and Uncle Don reach the cabin about the same time. "Uncle Don, look what I found on my way back to the cabin. I'm hoping that they might give us some answers." "I sure hope so Sam. We sure could use a break on this one. I can't imagine someone deliberately doing something that would cause this to happen. I don't know maybe we better not eat these until we have them checked out." "Good idea. Let's take the fish to the lab and have them tested. I'll call John at the lab and he can meet us there when we get in.

"Ok, let's see who caught the biggest fish. Looks like I did Uncle Don. You're going to have to fix dinner." Uncle Don went into the kitchen to see what Mamie had sent along for them to eat. Great! Lunch meat, chips, tomatoes, and soft drinks. "Perfect! We can have sandwiches, chips and soda. Wait a minute, what's this? Good ole Mamie slipped in some apple pie and marshmallows. Here you go Sam. "Looks good Uncle Don. Why is it that sandwiches always taste better when you're out like this?" "I don't know but they sure do".

Sam had built a fire in the fireplace because at night the temperature tends to drop and it would get a little chilly. After eating Sam and Uncle Don talked for awhile. "Sure is peaceful out here." "It sure is." "Sam looks at the treat Mamie sent with them. "Marshmallows." "This is the life." Sam and Uncle Don roast their marshmallows. "I think it's a shame everyone can't enjoy life this way."

"Buy the way, tell me about the man I met the other night, the one they call Bear?" What do you think of him?" "A real personable character Huh?" "To say the least." Sam goes on to tell Uncle Don what she knows about him. "I'm glad he is going to help us, but you still haven't told me yet what you think of him." "I really don't know. I've really only known him for a couple of days." "I think this one is a keeper Sam." "Oh, Uncle Don, I don't need you trying to be a match maker. You know I don't like that." "Well you might want to give it some thought. We better get some sleep if we are going to head back in the morning. Good night Sam. "Good night Uncle Don."

Sam woke up early the next morning and put on the coffee for Uncle Don and fixed herself a cup of tea after she had the jeep all loaded up for their trip back home. Sam goes outside to take it all in, Mother Nature at her best. A small bunny hops over to where Sam was sitting in the green grass and she fed it some wild clover that was growing beside her. A fawn's curiosity gets the better of itself and wonders over to where Sammy was sitting with the bunny. A little ways over were some squirrels playing. Sam was having the time of her life. Uncle Don smelled the coffee and made his way into the kitchen when he noticed Sam through the window. She was chatting away to the bunny and fawn. He walked over to the door and watched for awhile until one by one they wondered away. Uncle Don had another cup of coffee and took it to the porch. "Good morning Sam." "Good morning Uncle Don." "Sam, how do you do it?" "Do what?" "You know, talk to the animals the way you do. You know everyone can't do that." "They could if their spirit was free." "What do you mean?" "Well, everyone seems to be caught up in all the problems around them, along with all the problems going on in their own life. They feel tense and worried about this or that and it sends out vibrations and the animals sense it. If people could relax, and trust in the Lord to help them, they could become one with nature and they could do it too.""Just like Adam and Eve, the way God intended it to be. You know how you can tell when people don't want to be bothered with or the people who just have bad attitudes. We tend to stay away from them. The

animals sense this in us and can tell if they can
trust us or if they need to stay clear." "Really!"
Really!"

"I'm going to call John so he can meet us
as soon as we get there. Sam did you notice
some men on a raft while you were fishing
yesterday?" No why?" Yesterday I noticed two
men floating on a raft on the lake on my way
back to the cabin. They seemed out of place to
me for some reason. I don't know maybe it was
my imagination running away with me." Uncle
Don makes the call and they head for home.

"Uncle Don did the paper say what
department the job opening was in?" Yes, the
receiving department." "Good, then we should
be able to keep a close eye on what is going
on from there. Here we are back home again."

"Uncle Don, if you don't mind going to the
lab alone I'd like to stay here and get my paper
work ready for tomorrow so I can apply for that
job. Call me later and let me know what you
find out." "Ok Sam, talk to you later." "We'll
have to do this again sometime." "Yeah, that
would be great. It was a lot of fun." Sam took
the fish into Mamie and told her not to fix them
until she hears back from Uncle Don. She
explained why and put them into the freezer
after she cleaned them and packed them in

The Emerald Ring

ice.

Chapter 4: The Interview

Sam headed for her room and jumped into the shower. When she finished her shower she saw Baby waiting for her in front of the bed. "Hi Baby, how's my girl?" *Let me see, what should I wear tomorrow? I guess I'll wear a suit. Since the job opening was in the receiving department I'll probably be interviewed by a man so I'd better look good. I know, I'll wear my blue suit with the black trim and my black heels will be perfect.* Sam lays out her clothes for in the morning.

The phone rang, It's Uncle Don. "What did you find out?" "Well the fish did have something in them but not at a level harmful to humans." "We'd better call the department of health and report it to them and they can take it from here." "Ok?" "See you later Uncle Don."

Sam went into her private computer room and got her paper work ready to take with her for the next morning. *Ok, this should be enough to qualify for any job they have.* Sam left the room and crawled onto the bed. She gave the bed a pat and Baby jumped up with her. Sam lies there thinking about the kiss Bear gave her and then she fell asleep.

The Emerald Ring

The alarm went off and Sam hurried along to get her exercises over with. She jumped into the shower and got dressed. She put on enough make-up to give her a soft gentle look. Sam looked into the mirror to check her eye make-up. "Yep, just right." Sam did have beautiful eyes and even more so when she highlighted them. They had a way of talking to you without saying a word. "Ok now I'm ready."

Sam headed for the kitchen to have breakfast before she left. "Well Mamie, how do I look?" "Oh Sammy you look so beautiful. When they see you coming you're going to knock them over." "Wish me luck Mamie." "I will, but as always you won't need it." Sam drove into town and found the Janex Corporation building. *Impressive*, she thinks to herself. On her way into the building she stopped a minute and asked a nice looking gentleman for directions to the personnel office. Captivated by her beauty he escorted her to the office personally. "Thank you for your assistance." "My pleasure Mam. Let me introduce myself, my name was Sterling McFadden. If you need anything or I can be of any help please call me. Here is my card."

Sam being polite put the card into her purse. Sam filled out the application and filled in the references and asked for an interview. Judy in personnel placed a call to Jack Anderson, the Supervisor in the receiving department. Mr. Anderson informed her that he would be there in a minute.

Meanwhile Sterling was in his office checking to see if there was anything in the executive office for her. He found out that their receptionist had just walked out on them to get married. Sterling quickly called down to personnel and had security escort her to his office. Judy in personnel told her to go with security so she went with him. On the way to the elevator the men are doing double takes as she walks by and Sam just smiled.

Sam noticed that Jack Anderson's office was on the second floor by the directory in the elevator. The security officer keyed the elevator to go to the seventh floor. Sam asked the officer why he had keyed the elevator to go to seven. Sam explained to him that she was supposed to be going to the second floor for an interview with Jack Anderson in the receiving department. "I've been ordered to take you to the executive office." "I don't understand, I thought I was going to be interviewed by a Mr. Anderson."

"I don't know, all that I was told was to

bring you to Mr. McFadden's office." Sam
noticed his name on his uniform, Joe. Sam
said, "Joe who is Mr. McFadden?" "He owns
the company and is the President of the
Corporation." "I see, said Sam." Joe told Sam
to follow him and that he would take her to his
office. "Here you are good luck. If you need
anything just pick up the phone and have the
operator page me. Don't forget my name is
Joe."

Mr. McFadden's secretary told her to go on
in that he was expecting her. Confused she
goes on in and walks over to the desk. There
was a man standing behind the desk looking
out of the window. When the man turned
around she noticed that it was the same man
that had escorted her to the personnel office.
"Mr. McFadden you wanted to see me?" "Yes,
when I got to my office this morning my
secretary informed me that my receptionist had
quit to go and get married. I remembered
walking you to personnel and I called to see if
maybe you would be interested in working for
me." "Oh, I see. What does this job require me
to do?"

"My receptionist does need computer
experience because she will be working with
me putting in vital information. She will have to

be able to pull up and get me information at a moment's notice. Computer experience is a must for this job." "What else would I do?" "Answer phones; help my secretary Jean when she needs help. Do you think you would be interested in the job?" "Maybe." Mr. McFadden told her that salary is no problem and that the benefits are excellent." That's good." After negotiating for awhile Sam accepted the job. "See you first thing in the morning. Just call me Sterling." Ok." "Then you can call me Sam." "Ok." Sam left for home.

Sterling had Jean, his secretary, order fresh flowers for her desk to be delivered every day after she had left. Sterling, was a very distinguished looking gentleman, standing six foot tall, weighing two hundred twenty five pounds with silverfish gray hair with blue eyes. He had a soft spoken voice and Sam didn't know it yet but Sterling had just fallen in love with her. Love at first sight. Looks like Sam is in for a little bit of trouble now. Not only did Sam have Bear trying to win her over, the President of the Janex Corporation was too. Sam's life was getting ready to become very complicated.

Sam arrived home and called her Uncle Don to let him know how the job went." Great Sam. I guess you know Sterling must have his eye on you." "Well, he will just have to look elsewhere. I'm really not interested in having a man in my life right now." "Oh Sam it would do you good. Ok, at least if he acts interested in you be friendly with him until we get what we need." "I guess I can for awhile. Uncle Don. You know I don't like playing those kinds of games. I have Baby and Star and I'm financially set, so I do not need anything else." "You're probably right. Speaking of reaching out, why don't you invite Bobbie out to go riding with you sometime? said Sam Well... what's wrong with Bobbie?" "Not a thing." "So, I'm not ready share my life yet." "Neither am I". "Ok point well taken. I'll think about it ok." "Ok. Now how about you Sam?" "Well I'm not going to think about it too much,but I will promise not to be so closed minded about it. Deal?"

Sam went to her room to take a short nap and Mamie calls her on the intercom. "Sam, it's Bear on the phone." Ok Mamie." "Hello." Hi Stuff, I thought I'd check in with you and see when you wanted to get together this week." "Let me think about that. I started working today at the Janex Corporation." "You did!" "Yeah." "WOW that's great."

"I went in to apply for a job in the receiving department and ended up with a job in the executive office." "I'm impressed." "Can you believe it I'm a receptionist for Sterling, the President of the company." "Sam you be careful. You're in a great spot to get the information we need but if you get caught it could be dangerous. Sam, don't forget you can call me anytime if you need me." "Thanks Bear. You know, now that I have met Sterling, it is hard to believe he has anything to do with this." "You never know Sam." "Let's get together Saturday afternoon." Sounds like a plan to me. See you later Stuff." "Bye Bear."

Mamie called Sam for supper and they talked about her new job. "This man Sterling, I think he has his eye on you so you had better be careful." "You think so Mamie? He seems so nice." "Well just take it one day at a time. Sam don't forget about Bear. He seems like a nice man too. Remember you are there to catch the bad guys." "I know Mamie, I'll be careful." "How was Bear when he called?" "Well he wasn't mushy or anything like that if you are wondering." "He was probably playing it cool because he doesn't know how you feel about him yet. He will probably wait for a signal from you before he makes his next move." Good. I'm going out to the stable to see Star." "Ok Sam." "Oh Mamie, Bear is coming out Saturday afternoon." "Great!"

Chapter 5: On the Job

"Hi Star, how is my big boy?" Sam starts brushing Star and starts thinking about Bear and the moment they looked into each other's eyes. It was like we were being drawn together. "Well Star I am a working girl now. What do you think about that?" Star shakes his head no. "Come on Star it will be ok. You know I wouldn't forget about you. I'd better go and get ready for bed so I can get up for work in the morning. I love you Star." Off to her room she went. Sam laid out what she was going to wear in the morning and took her shower. Sam put on her pj's and jumped into bed. Sam patted the bed for Baby and she jumped up. "Hi baby girl, guess what next week is? Next week end is when I take you to visit your friend." Sam played with her awhile and they both fell asleep.

Once a month Sam takes Baby to the zoo to play with her friends. Sam started taking Baby to the zoo when she was just a cub.

When the alarm went off Sam did her exercises and jumped into the shower. Then she got ready for work. Mamie called her to breakfast." Good luck today Sam, I really don't think you need it."

Janet McBaine

When Sam got to work she found fresh flowers on her desk. Sam was impressed. She looked at the card in the flowers. It was from Sterling. The card said, *"Beautiful flowers for a beautiful lady, you're like a breath of fresh air, just what this place needs. Hope you have a nice day,"* signed Sterling. Oh, that is really nice. Sam sat down at her desk and familiarized herself with everything. The phone rings and it is Sterling." Good morning sir." "Good morning Sterling. Sam." "I mean good morning Sterling." "That's better." "Thank you for the flowers, that was really nice of you." "I'm glad you like them. I should be there in about 30 minutes. Just take messages until I get there and I will show you around the place."

After taking several messages Sterling arrived. "Mr. McFadden." He looks at her." I mean Sterling, here are you messages." He said, "Thanks Sam" as he looked through them. He headed for his office and told Sam that he would be right back. Sterling returned in about 10 minutes. "Ok Sam, are you ready to go?" "I guess." "The first thing I'm going to show you is where everyone is located." Sam had already met his secretary Jean so he introduced her to all the managers of the floors. "The most important thing to remember is that no one is allowed up here except the managers and even they have to call first." "Ok. I'll remember." "Do you have any questions?" "Not right now."

"Let's get your password to your computer from Jean." "Ok." "Jean takes care of all my typing, the filing and setting up of appointments for us. If someone wants to set up an appointment transfer them to Jean. Jean has worked here for twenty years and knows all the ups and downs of this place. If you need any help with anything just ask Jean. She won't mind helping you. Actually I've only been here myself a year and she has been a life saver to me. I don't know what I would have done without her. She has helped me a lot. So you see I'm kind of new to this company too. Jean is going to train you so now I'm going to leave you in her good hands."

Jean explained the phone system to her and how to reach everyone in the building. Sam caught on quickly and Jean was amazed at how fast she learned everything. Jean told Sam, "I'm very impressed with your skills with the computer. Sam I wouldn't be surprised if there are things that you could show me." Boy if she only knew. "The girl that worked here before would help me when I would get swamped with things." "I'd be glad to help you

Jean." "Just let me know and we'll have it done in no time." "Thanks Sam." It's getting close to lunch so I am going to let you relax a minute and get used to everything. I'll get back to you in a little while to see how you are doing."

At lunch time Sterling showed up and asked Sam if she had made any plans for lunch yet. Sam told Sterling that she hadn't. Sterling replies, "good, if you wouldn't mind I'd be honored if you would join me for lunch." "Me?" "Yes you. So, how about it Sam?" "I guess it would be ok." Jean looked at Sam and gave her the ok sign and smiled. She started thinking about what Uncle Don had told her.

"Sam where would you like to go to lunch?" "I guess that all depends on how much time we have. You're with me so today we will not worry about time." Ok then I don't care, surprise me." "Ok." Sterling took her to an oriental restaurant not very far from work. Sam's thinking to herself, *being nice to Sterling is going to be easy.* They talked for awhile until they started feeling more comfortable and then they headed back to work. "Sam is all yours now Jean." "Ok Mr. McFadden."

Jean told Sam "Go for it." Sam asked, "Go for what?" "Mr. McFadden." "Sterling? What do you mean?" "He lost his wife right after he took

The Emerald Ring

over this company and he's had a hard time of it. He's really a nice man and I think you are just what he needs right now." "I'm happy just the way I am." You're lucky. Most women your age and even my age panic if they do not have a man in their life." "I know but that's silly."

"You don't have to have a man in life to be happy. It is ok to be single. Happiness is a state of mind. If you find someone who wants to share your life with them and can share your dreams with you and respect the things you believe in, then that's great. Your life can be richer and you can reach a point in life where love is so special and the both of you can reach a closeness with God that's so unbelievable. There are no words to describe it. "

"I know some women that have a man in their life and they are so miserable. I just don't understand. Why have a man in your life if he's going to make you so unhappy. That's not the way God planned it. If a man can bring joy, happiness, and add a spark of inward mischievousness in you out; and a since of oneness between you, then you have a match made in Heaven. I also know you don't find that kind of love very often. The main reason we don't find that kind of love is that we really do not know what we are looking for. When a guy pays a little attention to us we say this is it. Later we find out that the relationship wasn't meant to be. We find ourselves just excepting the relationship because we don't know how to get out of it. I do know it exists; I had it once upon a time. I've learned to appreciate life and what it has to offer. So many people take things for granted. Most people don't even realize what they have until it's too late."

"All I'm saying Sam is just give him a chance. Ok. I know that being single can be great and I'm happy for you. I'm not asking you to fall in love with him. Just enjoy his company for awhile and see what happens. Alright, he does seem like a nice man."

Sterling came by before he left work to see Sam. "Do I have any messages?" "No." "How did you like your first day?" "It was alright." "Tomorrow when you come in we'll work with the computer. I know Jean has shown you a few things but tomorrow we'll get down to business." Ok" "See you tomorrow Sam."

Mamie had supper ready when Sam got home." How's it going Sam?" "Pretty good actually. Mamie I think you are right about " "Sterling took me to lunch today. He's really nice Mamie. I just can't believe that he is involved in this mess." "Maybe he isn't and it is someone else in the company. Maybe he doesn't know what is going on." "I sure hope you're right. Tomorrow they are teaching me their computer system. Sterling is teaching me himself personally." "Well now." Mamie thinks to herself, *they don't have a clue what that little gal can do with a computer and chuckles to herself.*

"I'm going out to see Star for awhile Mamie." Ok." The phone rings. It's Uncle Don. "How is it going Sam? "You and Mamie were right about one thing, at least according to his secretary Jean. Sterling had flowers on my desk when I got there this morning and he took me to lunch, so I guess he might be interested in me. He even enclosed a card." "Great. This is are going to be better than we planned. This position is even better than the one you went to apply for. You'll be able to get a lot more information. You will have a better chance of checking things out without much trouble." "What did you find out Uncle Don?" "Nothing yet. I'm checking out the employees with Bear at the police station." "Bear is coming out here Saturday afternoon and we're getting together to see what we have come up with by then." "Ok Sam if Bear is seeing you on Saturday why don't you and I get together on Friday." "Sure but before you see me on Friday make sure you call Bobbie to see if she has found out anything before we meet." "Ok, talk to you later."

Sam went out to the stable to see Star for awhile. After spending some time with Star Sam went back in the house to get ready for bed. Baby jumped up in bed with her and they drifted off to sleep.

Sam wakes up. Wow, it's Wednesday morning already. This week sure is going by fast. After exercising, showering and hurrying her breakfast down she headed for work. "See you later Mamie." "Good luck Sam and please be careful." "I will"

Sam went to the office early and since she had her password to the computer she started snooping to see what she could find out. After about a half an hour, Sam felt confident that when the time came she would be able to retrieve whatever she needed. Sam shuts off the computer and answered the phone. Flower delivery. Sam asked them to contact security since it was to be delivered to the executive floor. Sam remembered that no one was to be allowed to come to the seventh floor without permission or a security escort.

The Emerald Ring

Minute's later security delivers a flower arrangement to Sam." Who are they from?" The delivery man said he was supposed to deliver fresh flowers to the executive department every day to Sam." Who are they from? O my goodness." A few minutes later Sterling walks in. "Good morning Sam. Do I have any messages?" "No, but I need to talk to you. "Sure Sam what is it?" "When I came to work yesterday, I found flowers on my desk and I thought that was very nice. Now here is another delivery and from what I understand I will be getting them every day. I don't understand. I don't know what to say." "Just say thank you and let it go at that." "Sterling you just don't send flowers to someone you work with every day." "Why not? I can do whatever I want to, I own the company. You're a beautiful lady and a beautiful lady needs flowers. Look at it this way, you can think of them as good public relations. It creates a good atmosphere for when people come in for a meeting or whatever the reason." "Yes sir. Thank you and I will enjoy them." "I have a meeting at 10:00, after that we'll work with the computer." "Ok." Sam thinks to herself, *boy could I show you a thing or two about your computer.* In the meantime several calls came in for Mr. McFadden and Jean had Sam type up some memos for her. "I really appreciate your help." "I don't mind. Ask me anytime."

Sterling came out of his office and asked Sam if he had any messages. "Yes sir." "Yes what?" "Yes Sterling." "That's better. See you at lunch." "Lunch?" said Sam."You are going to have lunch with me today aren't you?" "Well, I don't know, I guess." "Great. It sure is a beautiful day Sam." "If you say so." "Oh Sam, if a Mr. Taylor calls for me, tell him that I'm out of town and will be checking in with you sometime today." "Ok." "Oh and Sam, I've called for a meeting of all the managers but it will be over by noon."

Jean walked over to Sam. "I don't know what you did to him but whatever it was keep up the good work. I've never seen him like this before." Sterling made sure that the meeting was over by 11:45 so that he could take Sam to lunch. Sterling picked up some papers from Jean and told Sam that he would be with her in a minute. "I just need to put these papers on my desk."

While Sam was waiting for Sterling to drop the papers off on his desk Bear calls her." Hi Sam, I'm just checking on you to make sure you are ok." "That is really thoughtful Bear."

The Emerald Ring

"To answer your question yes I'm fine and everything was ok." "Great." Sterling walked over to Sam and asked her if she was ready for lunch. "I'll be ready in a minute." "Thanks for calling. I'll talk to you later ok? I've got to go now." "Ok Stuff, but remember if you need me, call me anytime." "I will but don't worry." "Ok Sterling I'm ready." "Where would you like to go?" "I don't care." "Jean where can we have lunch? "The Haden House was a good place to eat." "The Haden House it is." Sterling walked over to Jeans desk and asked her to make reservations for him for lunch every day. "You got it Mr. McFadden. Don't worry about a thing. "Off they went. "Sterling I really enjoyed having lunch with you yesterday. It was nice. It's been a long time since I've had so much fun. I really enjoyed your company." "Really?" "Do you think maybe you would have dinner with me some evening?" "I don't know about that." "Do you already have a boyfriend? Listen to me of course you do someone as pretty as you." "No, it's not that. I just don't date anyone right now." "You don't. Why not? Someone as pretty as you should have the phone ringing off the hook." "My phone number is unlisted. I'm not ready to have anyone in my life right now." "Are you enjoying yourself right now?" "Yes I am." "Sam at least give me a fighting chance.""Ok let me think about it for awhile." "Ok." "Lunches are fine for now."

Sterling told her, "You know I'm not going to give up on you." "Fair enough. We'd better get back to work, you are supposed to show me the computer this afternoon, remember? "I remember but I'd rather stay here with you. When I'm with you I forget all about the rat race out there. You're such a breath of fresh air and it is such a delight to have you around." "Don't you think you are moving kind of fast? "I" don't know and frankly I do not care. All I know is that I count the minutes until I'm going to see you again." "Here we are. My computer awaits.

"Let's forget the computer and go and enjoy the rest of the day." "We can't do that. This is my job." "Yes we can. I'm the boss. Jean can handle anything that would come up. "It is tempting but now it is time to come back to the real world. Sterling to Earth." "Oh alright if you insist. You can't blame me for trying. I told you I'm not going to give up."

Sterling showed her the computer system for their office and was impressed at how fast Sam caught on to everything. A call came in and it was for Sterling.

Sterling took the call in his office. After he

talked on the phone for a few minutes he came out and told Sam that he was going to be out of town for a few days. "Jean, I need to get a plane ticket," and he wrote down all the things he needed for her to do. "I'll take care of it sir." "Thanks Jean." "Sam maybe we can have dinner when I get back. Well, at least think about it." Sterling gathered up some papers and was on his way out the door.

Jean came over to Sam and tried to talk her into going out to dinner with him. "Don't you find him attractive?" "Yes, he is very handsome." "Come on "I really don't want to talk about it." What is there to think about?" Jeans phone rings and she heads back to her desk. Sterling had given Sam a few things to put into the computer. Sam logged everything in and notices that it was finally 5 o'clock. Time to go. On her way home she kept thinking about how complicated her life was starting to become. *I need to talk to Mamie. Sterling is definitely interested in me and there's no doubt about that. He had made that perfectly clear. Then there is Bear, he's quite a hunk and he did say that I was cute the other night. I wonder just how interested in me he is. If Bear is really interested in me then what am I going to do about Sterling?*

Janet McBaine

Home at last. Sam goes into the kitchen and Mamie greets her. "How was your day Sammy?" "Mamie I need some help. I'm getting so confused." "What are you so confused about?" "Men, I just don't know what to do. Sterling laid it out on the line exactly how he feels about me today. Mamie, he has only known me a couple of days and he is moving so fast it scares me. I have fresh flowers on my desk every morning and when he gets back he wants me to go to dinner with him. I told him that I would think about it." "What about Bear Sam?" "I know. What do I do?" "Isn't Bear supposed to come out here Saturday?" "Yes." "Maybe after you see him you'll be able to sort it out better." "I sure hope so Mamie. I really enjoy being with Sterling, he makes me laugh and we have so much fun together. I like that. I don't get the same feeling with Sterling as I do with Bear. I get a warm feeling all over when I'm with Bear and I feel like I am sixteen again. You see Mamie this is why I don't like getting involved with someone. It tears your nerves up. Life gets so confusing and frankly I just don't know if it is worth it. I guess I'll just take it one day at a time."

Sam went into her room to change before dinner. She walked over to her bed and laid down across her pillows. *Oh Jimmy, why did*

The Emerald Ring

you have to die? We had so much going for us. Letting you go was the hardest thing that I've ever had to do. I can still remember that sound of the Heart monitor at the hospital the night that they rushed me out of your room only to come back and tell me that you were gone. My whole world seemed to stop at that moment. I don't know what I would have done if it weren't for Star. He helped me get through it. Star was born the night you died. his mother died giving birth to him. We bonded that night. I took care of him until he could make it on his own. I guess that is why he is so close to me now. You would have liked him Jimmy. He was definitely a one of a kind.

Mamie called her to come and eat. Sam sat down at the table and Mamie asked her what was wrong? "Oh, I was just remembering Jimmy." "I see. You shared a lot of good times together Sam. A lot of good memories to hang on to." "I know Mamie and I cherish each one of them. I don't think I could stand to go through losing another one of them. "Dying is a part of life we all have to deal with at some time in our lives. With God's help we move on and learn to take each day as it comes. We learn to make the best of each day so that we have no regrets. Sammy." "Why did you give me such a strange look when I said that?" "I have heard that phrase before when describing someone we both know". "Who Sam?" "Bear."

The phone rings. It's Bear. "Hello." "Hi stuff. Are you ok?" "Yes why?" "I don't know I just sensed that you needed me." "You did." "Yes. I've learned to listen to my senses. They are usually right and when it comes to you I'm not taking any chances." "Bear I don't know what to say. It's nice having someone to look out for me. It has been awhile since someone did that. I really appreciate you calling me. I'm feeling much better now. Is there anything I can do?" "No, it is just going to take time. What do they say, time heals all wounds. A few years ago I lost someone very special to me and tonight it was weighing heavy on me." "I'm sorry Sam." "Thanks Bear." "Do you like picnics Sam?" Yes, why?" "Well when I come over Saturday why don't you and I go on a picnic? Would you like that?" "I think that would be nice Bear. I'll have Mamie fix us a picnic lunch and we can ride up to the lake and have our picnic." "Sounds like a plan to me Stuff, see you Saturday." "Ok."

"Mamie, would you mind fixing up a picnic basket for Bear and I on Saturday? We're going to ride up to the lake and have a picnic." Mamie says, "I think that is just what you need right now." "I know, says Sam." "This could end up being a special day for you Sam." "Yeah, you could be right Mamie. He said the reason he called was that he sensed that I needed him. How did he know?"

Sam went back into her room and laid across her bed. *No one will ever be able to take Jimmy's place but maybe Bear is the one to help me move on with my life. Oh Bear, I sure hope you are the one. I have got to admit I do think about you a lot. I feel safe when you are around. I can't believe he wants to take me on a picnic. There must be a gentle side to him. He must really be in tune with me if he sensed that there was something wrong with me tonight. Maybe he does care for me if he can sense that. I sure hope he does. Look at me. I can't believe what I am thinking. Yesterday I didn't care about a relationship in my life at all and today I'm hoping that Bear wants to be a part of it. I have Sterling who is insisting on being a part of it. I don't know maybe it is time. I think I'll go and check on Star before I get ready for bed.*

Sam checked on Star and called her Uncle Don. "Hi Uncle Don." "Hi Sam. What's up?" "I wanted to let you know that Sterling is going to be out of town for a couple of days." "Sam you be careful." "I will." "I'll have the whole day to look into the computer and try to make heads or tails out of what is going on." "Have you and Bear come up with anything yet?" "Not yet but I'll know more when I meet you for lunch on Friday. I did see Shamrock the other day and he told me that he got a job driving the trucks and making deliveries." "Great! I hope we can wrap this up in a hurry. I called Bobbie and she is going to get back with me tomorrow. It looks like those names you got from Tina at the court house might tie into this somehow." "Really? I'd better start checking on the employees first and see how they might tie in together. At least that's a start. Maybe by the time we meet for lunch we may have something to go on."

Sam got ready for bed and started thinking about the big job ahead of her. *Why is there a list of employees from the Janex Corporation at the court house? The answer has got to be in the computer. If it is there I'll find it. Tomorrow I'll leave my computer on and if I find anything I can transfer the information straight to my computer. That way I never have anything on me. I wonder if Jean knows anything. I'll see what I can find out from her. If there is anything going on I'll bet she knows about it or at least suspects something and can't do anything about it. I'd better be careful until I know where she stands. I don't think*

The Emerald Ring

Jean was the kind of person that would let anything illegal go on unless her hands were tied.

The next morning Mamie called Sam for breakfast. Sam did her daily routine. Then she got dressed and had her breakfast. Mamie reminded Sam to be careful because she knew how intent Sam could be in finding some evidence that they could use. She might be too focused on the computer and not hear someone coming up on her. "I'll be careful Mamie. I just hope I can find something." "Good luck Sam." Sam drove off and headed for work. Sam was thinking that Jean would probably come in late for work today because she knew I'd be there to cover her since Sterling was out of town.

Sam looked around and it was just as she suspected, no one there. *This just might be the break I need to find something. Sam looked on Sterling's calendar and saw a lunch date with Sam. I wonder if Jean had canceled this. If she hadn't maybe I can go and feel her out and see what she knows.*

Chapter 6: Gathering The Evidence

Sam went over to her desk and had just sat down when the phone rang. It's Shamrock. "I am at the loading dock Sam." "Shamrock what is it?" "I'm being sent out on a special run today and I think this could be the break that we have been looking for." "Great." "You be careful and get back to me as soon as you can. Ok Sam."

Jean arrived at 8:30 am. "Good Morning Sam, anything going on?" "No not a thing." Sam turned on her computer and started to enter some things into the computer. Jean walked over to her desk and asked Sam to cover for her awhile. "Sure Jean no problem." *I wonder what she is up to. I sure hope she is not involved in this. Now's my chance to do some checking. Let's see, here is a list of employees. I'll pull them up and see how many people have been here for ten years. Now let's see how many people have been transferred here in the last fifteen years. Interesting. All the names on the list are here. Now let me see how I can tie them together.* The phone rings. It is Shamrock. "Can you talk?" "Yes, what is it." "Bingo. We have the evidence we've been

The Emerald Ring

looking for." "Great! How?" "My boss had me take several drums up to Canyon Lake early this morning before anybody else started. Just in case I put several empty drums on the truck and drove where I could fill them up with water so I could exchange them in case we had something." "Good thinking Shamrock. Why did they have you take them to the lake?" "They told me to empty them into the lake. So I emptied the ones I had filled with water and hid the ones we need for evidence." "Good work Shamrock. Now what?"

"I'm going to try to send what evidence I can find in the computer to the one I have at home." "Can you do that?" "I can with my set up." "Wow! I'm supposed to pick up the drums I left in a couple of days so we have a little time. "Ok. If you hear anything else let me know. You better be careful Shamrock. "I will. You do the same. "

Sam entered each name in the computer and asked the computer who hired each one. They were all hired by the same man, interesting. *Now what?* Sam looked to see which department they worked in. *Ok we have some working in shipping, receiving, accounting, the dock area and quality management. I see they have someone in each department so that they can cover their tracks. How clever.*

Sam pulls up another screen. *Now, let me see, where do I want to go from here? Here's something I definitely want to look into.* Sam figures out how to get into the screen. *Ok now. What do we have here? Canyon Lake. Ok. Sent man to lake from dock to dispose of four drums of chemicals. Note: Inspection tomorrow. I wonder what kind of inspection it is? There must be a memo on it somewhere. It's getting close to lunch time. I wonder if Jean will make it back before lunch.* Sam downloaded everything she had found to her computer at home and logged off.

Sam got caught up on the things she had on her desk just when Jean walked in. "Hi Jean! Are you ready for lunch?" "Yes I am." "I haven't made any plans yet. Do you want to have lunch together?" "Sure that sounds great. Where do you want to eat?" "I haven't canceled the reservation for you and Sterling yet; want to go there? We'll have lunch on him today. "Sounds good to me." Off they went to lunch.

"How do you like working for Janex Sam? "I really like it and everyone is so nice. I hope I still like it in a couple of years. Usually by that time I've learned all about the company and its politics I'm ready to leave." "What do you mean?" "You know when you find out how the company really feels about their employees. They pretend to have their best interest at heart but when it comes to benefits and raises then it is another story. They give the same excuses all the time about how much it cost to expand and the cost of running the company are much higher than the year before and how they are losing money. They do a good job of covering up by the way they answer your questions. That is what they get paid for. "I know Sam. I've seen and heard it all." "What do you mean?" "Over the last ten years I've seen a drastic change in the company." "How?"

"There was a time when you really felt like coming to work because you felt like you were a member of a team. Everybody worked hard and helped each other and didn't mind doing it. Now if you get caught helping someone you get a lecture on it like you committed some kind of crime or something. I just don't understand why people have to be that way. Well there is a reason behind all of it." "Well I don't know what in the world it could be." "There are a lot of things going on in the company that they do not want the employees to know about." "Like what?" "It's best you don't know Sam." "I'm bound to find out sooner or later Jean." "Sterling has me logging things in the computer all the time and I'm not a dummy." "I know but the last girl that worked your job was and didn't care." "is it illegal?" "Let's put it this way, it is not on the up and up." "I see. Can we get into trouble if they get caught?" "I don't think so." "is Sterling a part of this?" "As far as I can tell he isn't." "I'm glad to hear that." "Our jobs really don't get involved with it so they can't say we are a part of it." "Are you going to tell me what they are doing?" "No I don't think so; it is for your own protection. I wouldn't want anything to happen to you." "I really appreciate that Jean." "Well I guess we had better hurry back to the office." "I guess so." "This was fun, I'm glad we had a chance to spend some time together." "Me too."

Chapter 7: Up in Smoke

As soon as they got back to the office Sam got a phone call from Sterling. "Hi Sam is there anything going on that I should know about?" "No everything is quiet." "When are you coming back?" "Tomorrow night or sometime Saturday. Can I call you when I get back?" "I'm going to be pretty busy this weekend so I'll see you on Monday. You have a safe trip home." Ok Sam." "Jean, that was Sterling. He said he would be back sometime Friday night or Saturday." "Thanks Sam." Sam busied herself with some odds and ends on her desk. Shamrock called Sam to see how things were going. "So far so good Shamrock, now you be careful." "I am. Don't worry about me. I'll talk to you later Sam." Ok." "Jean I'm going after the mail now. Do you want me to do anything for you?" No, I'm fine. Thanks anyway." Sam headed for the mail room.

On her way to the mail room she noticed some men standing by the elevators and overheard them talking about Shamrock. They did not see her because she hid behind some tall plants. *Oh my goodness. I've got to warn Shamrock. I wonder if he is at the dock.* Sam walked over to the house phone and called the dock. She asked for Shamrock. They told her that he was out in the truck running errands and asked if they could take a message. "No that's ok." *I've got to get a hold of Bear so he can warn Shamrock.* Sam went to the pay phone in the lobby and called Bears pager number. Bear called her right back. "Bear I've only got a minute, listen carefully. Shamrock has two drums that we can use as evidence and they have found out about it. I overheard two men talking a few minutes ago about how they were going to have to take him out. You have got to warn him. He is in the Janex truck." "Ok Sam. I can take it from here." "You be careful." "You don't have much time it was 2:00 already. I get off in a couple of hours and I'll go straight home." "Call me as soon as you can. Ok. "

The next couple of hours seemed like it took forever before Sam could leave and go home. Sam told Jean that she would see her first thing in the morning. Sam headed for home hoping that by the time she got there she would hear from them. *I sure hope that Bear was able to get to Shamrock in time.*

After Sam contacted Bear he called on the radio and put a search out for Shamrock to try to locate him.

86

The Emerald Ring

Luckily another officer located him and contacted Beard over the radio. Bear advised him to stop him and hold him until he could get there. The officer pulled him over and Bear arrived shortly after he was pulled over. Bear pulled up and told the officer that he would take it from there. "Bear what is going on?" "They found out that you have those drums. Sam overheard them talking by the elevators." "What are we going to do now?" "I don't know yet. Let me think a minute. They'll be waiting for you when you get back to the dock. I know. My truck is parked where I could slip in and get out before they realized I was there." Good. Let's park the truck on the side and I'll follow you out to Sam's." "Ok." "We don't want to blow our cover so we will have to be real careful from now on. " Shamrock got into his truck and they headed for Sam's. Bear called Sam on his car phone and told her what was going on. "Sam, call your Uncle Don and Bobbie and have them meet us at your house. We need to talk about our next move." "Ok." "Mamie Bear is on his way here and he has Shamrock." "Oh praise the Lord." "I'm going to get hold of Bobbie and Uncle Don and have them come out here to see what we're going to do next. Whatever it is we are going to have to be very careful."

Mamie went into the kitchen and put on extra food. Sam came into the kitchen just as Shamrock and Bear got there. Mamie told Sam that she had supper ready. "Mamie I can always count on you. I didn't even think about supper." "Just as I thought, you guys have got to eat." Sam went to greet Shamrock and Bear at the door. "I sure am glad you are ok Shamrock. I've been so worried about you." Shamrock told them he didn't know what to think when the Police pulled him over. Bear smelled Mammies cooking in the air. "Yes Bear, Mamie has supper all ready and we can eat as soon as Uncle Don and Bobbie get here." Mamie walked in and Bear gave her a great big bear hug. "How's my sweetheart?" "Now Bear behave yourself" A car pulled up. "It's Uncle Don and he had Bobbie with him."

They all sat down at the dinner table and started discussing what they were going to do next. Each one told what they've learned so far. "Even with the physical evidence we have it still isn't enough to close them down. They would probably get off with just a stiff fine."

Bear and Sam started thinking that they might just be able to pull this off with Bobbie and Uncle Don's help, along with Shamrocks evidence. Bear and Uncle Don explained how they have been able to link the employees together in what was going on. While they all were discussing their next move Sam went into her computer room and printed off what she was able to get from the Janex Computer. It verified what Uncle Don and Bear were talking about. Sam showed Bobbie the papers in hopes that she might be able to use it in a legal standpoint. She explained how four drums of chemicals were taken from the dock up to Canyon Lake to be disposed of. "Thanks to Shamrock we now have those four drums in our possession. This paper shows that an inspection was to take place the next morning, The drums disappeared. I wonder what the connection is? It has to be linked together because of the threat to Shamrocks life. Some men found out that Shamrock hadn't taken the drums to the lake so they didn't want to take any chances and they were going to do away with him. I overheard them talking and called Bear right away and he took it from there. So here we are. "

"Whatever we do now had to be done with extreme caution. They are going to be watching now. Bobbie told them that she was going to start working on getting a petition to close them down." "I won't do anything until I hear from you guys giving me the go ahead."

Mamie came in and asked if anyone was ready for desert. Sam was not a dessert person. She had to be in the mood for it unless it was a special occasion. Uncle Don suggested that they all get together on Monday. "I think that is a good idea said Bear." Bear made sure that they all had his pager number. Bobbie suggested that they all keep in touch with each other at least until things cooled down. "It sounds like things could get pretty dangerous if we're not careful. What are we going to do with Shamrock?" "Those men are still looking for him." Bear asked Sam if Shamrock could stay with her for awhile or until he could figure out something else. Shamrock asks, "What about Pacos?" "I'll have Frank go over to your place and bring him back to the ranch. Ok?" "Are you sure you don't mind Sam?" "I don't mind but you better ask Mamie. She is the cook." "Well Mamie, do you mind feeding one more person for awhile?" "We'd be glad to have you Shamrock." "Thanks Mamie." Uncle Don gave Shamrock his pager number and told him if he needed help to call it and he would get Bear and head out here. "Great. Bobbie, I need to get going now." "Are you ready?" Mamie told Shamrock to follow her and she would show him to his room.

"Well, I guess that leaves us." "Yes, I guess

The Emerald Ring

it does." Sam and Bear walked out onto the patio by the pool. "Sam, I've never been afraid of anything in my life until now." "Bear are you afraid of these guys?" "These guys no. I'm not afraid of them, I'm just afraid they're going to hurt you and if that happens I'm going to have to kill someone." "You won't have to worry about closing them down." Then Bear looked at me with that Clark Gable smile of his. "Bear you can be so sweet." "I care Sam." "I'm beginning to see that." "Sam when you go to work tomorrow please be careful." "I will Bear. You don't have to worry about me. Really." "Sam I really don't think you know what you are getting yourself into." "Bear I've been in close spots before and I can take care of myself." "I know you think you can but you don't know what is out there." "Bear you don't understand. I am not some little girl who doesn't know what is going on. I can keep up with the best of them, trust me." "I am Sam, I am."

Mamie and Shamrock joined Bear and Sam on the patio. "Are you going to be alright Shamrock?" "I'll be ok Bear." "I don't know of anyone who would suspect to find me out here at Sam's place." "I don't either. Keep your eyes open just in case though. The biggest mistake you can make is underestimating your enemy." "10-4 good buddy." Shamrock bid them all a good night and told them that he was going to turn in. "It's been a long day." Sam walked Bear to his truck. "Sam if you want I can stay out here a little longer." "No you go ahead I'll be fine. I've got to get up early and go to work."

"I'll call you first thing in the morning to make sure everything is alright." "Ok. That would be nice." "See you later." Bear leaned over and kissed her on the forehead. On her way back to her bedroom she noticed Mamie and Shamrock were still chatting away. Sam thinks to herself, *Well look at you Mamie, you go girl.*

The alarm went off. *It can't be morning already. It seems like I just laid down.* Sam got dressed and ready for work. On her way to the kitchen she heard country music playing. *I can't believe what I am hearing; it was coming from the kitchen. That is not like Mamie.* When she walked into the kitchen Shamrock and Mamie were doing the two step. Sam said "Well get down. I can see you two are off to a good start." "Good morning Sam." "Good morning." Mamie told Sam that her breakfast was ready and they all sat down while Sam had her breakfast. Sam told Mamie and Shamrock not to get to carried away. "All kidding aside you be careful at work today." "I will." Sam started out the door when the phone rang. "Sam the phone is for you, it's Bear." "Ok Mamie." "Hello." "Hi Sam." "Hello Bear." I just called to make sure you were ok and to tell you to have a nice day." "That is really thoughtful and sweet. I'm just fine and I hope your day will be a good one too." "I can't wait until morning." What is going on in the morning Bear?" "We are going on a picnic remember?" "Oh, that's right. Do you still want to go since they're looking for Shamrock?" "Are you kidding? I wouldn't miss this picnic for anything in the world." "Oh Bear." "I'll call you later and check on you." "Ok. Bear." If you need me. I know, call you." "I will Bear." "See you later." "Bye." Sam headed out the door for work.

Sam thought about Bear all the way to work. It seemed like that was all she thought about lately.

Sam walked into her office and Jean hadn't arrived yet. Security delivered the daily flowers from her boss, *Sterling. Oh Sterling, what am I going to do with you? You're so sweet. I just can't make up my mind what to do. I sure do like you an awful lot. I have so much fun when we are together. When I'm with Bear I get a warm fuzzy feeling inside and I feel good all over.* The phone rings. It's Sterling. "Good

morning Sterling. I don't have any messages
for you." "That's ok I just wanted to hear you
voice anyway." "What am I going to do with you
Sterling? No don't answer that." When are you
coming back?" "I should be back late this
afternoon. If it's after 3:00 I will go on home
and unpack and pick you up at 7:00. Well that
would be nice but I have got company this
week end. I'll see you on Monday. Oh, just so
you know. I don't like people taking charge
when it comes to my life. This I'll come and
pick you up at 7:00 does not fly with me. You
check first and if I have time I'll let you know."
"I'm sorry. I guess you know that is going to
seem like a life time." "You'll survive." "I guess."
Jean came in and Sam told her that Sterling
had just called. "He said he should be in this
afternoon but if he wasn't here by 3:00 he was
going on home to unpack." "Ok thanks
Sam.""Did he seem to be in good spirits?" "As
a matter of fact he did." "Good. That means
that the deal he had been working on must
have gone through." "Is that good?" "It is for
the company but there are some that are not
going to be very happy. Sterling will be able to
do a little house cleaning around here now."
"What do you mean?" "He will be able to fire
some people that have not been on the up and
up around here at the company." "Why couldn't

he fire them before? He is the boss." "It's called politics. If the deal went through then the tables would be turned around in his favor and it would put him in the driver's seat." Great. "Sam, I'm going after the mail now." Ok Jean. I'll hold down the fort until you get back." Sam's phone rings and she answers it. It was Mr. Anderson, the dock foreman. "No. Mr. McFadden isn't in right now but is expected in this afternoon. Would you like to leave a message? I'm sure he'll get right back to you as soon as he comes in." "No, that won't be necessary. I'll check back with him later." "Ok." Sam made some coffee for Jean and to have it on hand in case someone dropped in. "Jean, Mr. Anderson just called for Sterling. I told him that he would be in this afternoon. He didn't want to leave a message." "Ok. I wonder what he wanted or what he is up to." "What do you mean what he is up to?" "Well he is one of the employees that Mr. McFadden has his eye on and really doesn't trust him. Sam would you help me type up some memos that need to go out on Monday?" "Sure Jean. Bring them over." Sam typed up five of the memos and ran copies of them so they would be ready to go out on Monday. "I'm going to take a break now Jean. I am finished with the memos and ran the copies so they are all good to go."

"Thanks." Sam headed for the dock and took one of the memos with her in case she needed some kind of cover up of while she was there. "I don't know why but I think there is something going on here. "*There was no paper work of any kind lying around here. No work orders, no orders. No nothing not even any employees. Something was definitely going on here.*

On her way back to the office she called Bear and told him what she had discovered. "You're right that doesn't sound good. You be careful." Sam headed back to her office and was just getting ready to sit down when the fire alarm went off. All of the elevators had gone to the first floor because of the alarm. Sam and Jean were on the top floor of the building. "Jean what are we going to do?" Jean says "It is probably a false alarm." "I don't think so Jean." They hear the overhead code 1000, second floor, dock area. The phone rings and it is Bear. "Sam I'm on my way. I just heard about the fire over my radio. Stay where you are. I'll come and get you. I should be there in about ten minutes." "Ok Bear." Sam relaxed a little more now that she knew help was on the way. It didn't seem like ten minutes when I looked up and there was Bear and another officer. They had keyed the elevator so that they could go up to get them. Bear grabbed her and gave her a great big Bear hug and asked her if she was alright. "Yes Bear, I'm fine. Bear you're shaking." "I know. I'll be alright now that I know you're ok." "Oh Bear, I guess that makes you my hero." "Ok Stuff, go ahead and tease me as long as I know you are ok." Jean told Bear to go ahead and take Sam home. "I don't think we are going to be getting much work done today." "Sounds good to me Jean. I'm out of here. "Bear told Sam that he was going to follow her home.

Mamie was getting ready to fix Shamrock some lunch when she saw Sam and Bear drive up. Mamie went running out. "Sam are you ok? What's wrong? Why are you home?"

"Everything is alright Mamie. There was a fire at the office and they sent everybody home that's all." "You two come on in and have some lunch." "Ok Mamie." "Hi Shamrock, how's it going?" "Great." "I bet it is," said Sam grinning. "I took Pacos for a ride around the ranch today and boy am I starved." Mamie fixed everybody some hamburgers. Sam and Bear filled them in on what went on at work today. "Sounds like things are getting pretty serious." Bear told them that he was going to investigate this fire himself. "I know the fire chief personally. Call your Uncle Don and tell him what happened.

Tell him that I'm going back to the Janex
building to start my investigation. If he wants to
meet me there I should be there for awhile.
Sam I'll check on you later." "Oh Sam what was
that little humor between you and Shamrock
when I asked him how things were going?" "I'll
tell you later. Ok.

   After Bear left Sterling called. Jean had
gotten a hold of him to let him know what had
happened. "Are you ok Sam?" "I'm alright
Sterling. How did you find out so fast?" "Jean
called me. She was lucky to catch me when
she did. Sam I'm coming out. I don't care if you
do have company or not. I have got to see
you." "Sterling." "I'm sorry Sam. I'm usually not
a pushy person. I just want to see and know
you are alright." "Ok Sterling but just for a little
while." "Thanks Sam." Sam gave him directions
on how to get to her ranch. In the meantime
Sam put Shamrock in her private room. "We
don't want to take any chances just in case. I'd
bet my life that he is clear of all this after
talking to Jean. It is always good to be safe
than sorry. I'll have Mamie check in on you but
Sterling shouldn't be here very long."

   It wasn't long before Sterling arrived. Sam
met him at the door. "Oh Sam, let me look at
you. It seems like a lifetime since I saw you.

The Emerald Ring

Let's go out on the patio." Ok." Sam you have a really nice place." "Thank you. My Grandfather left it to me when he died. I loved him very much, I sure miss him." Sterling took Sam in his arms and held her. "Sam why don't you give in. Let me take care of you?" "Now Sterling." "Ok I won't pressure you. At least I know you are alright and I did get to see you before Monday." They sat together for awhile not really saying anything. Sterling was holding her close as if he were afraid to let go. Afraid she would go away and he would never see her again. "Sterling, I think I'm going to get ready for bed. I have a long day tomorrow." "Ok Sam. I'll leave but not willingly. Thank you for letting me come over tonight. It meant a lot to me. It was very thoughtful of you and you know I always enjoy your company. I really appreciate you spending time with me." Sam reminds him that people are probably trying to reach him. "They probably are but my lady you are top priority in my life right now. I guess I'd better get back to Janex." Sam laughs a little. What am I going to do? She puts her finger over his lips. "I know." Sterling gives her a good night kiss and an embrace that would melt your heart.

Chapter 8: The Picnic

Sam went to her bedroom and let
Shamrock out of her private hidden room.
"Sam, this room is totally awesome. I hope you
don't mind I did a little Target shooting while I
was in there. You told me to make myself at
home." "That's ok Shamrock. The room is
sound proof. I figured that. is everything ok?"
"Yes." "Then why do you look like you just lost
your best friend?" Sterling just left." "And?"
"Well I really like him a lot but it's just not the
same way I feel when I'm around Bear." "And
how is that?" "I feel warm all over and I get all
nervous inside." "Sounds like you are in love to
me." "With Bear?" "Yes with Bear." "I think Bear
likes me. I've seen several signs and he did
say he cared the other day." "Sam let me tell
you something. Bear is so much in love with
you it is all he can do to hold it inside. He just
doesn't want to make the wrong move and end
up losing you." "Are you sure?" "Trust me. I
know Bear." "I sure hope you're right
Shamrock.   Bear will be here first thing in the
morning. We're going on a picnic." "You had
better get ready for bed if I know Bear; he will
be here when the sun pops up over the horizon
unless you told him a specific time. He did that

to me one morning." Sam got ready for bed and thought about the two of them. *If I get involved with Bear then I won't be able to spend time with Sterling anymore. I guess I'll just have to wait until tomorrow and see what happens.*

Saturday morning Bear arrives at Sam's. Mamie met Bear at the door. "Good morning Mamie." "Good morning Bear." "How's my favorite lady?" "Oh Bear. I've got your picnic lunch ready and I put in a homemade apple pie just for you." "Thanks Mamie, you're the greatest. I guess you know I'm quite taken with you girl.""I kind of figured that." "Do you think I have a chance Mamie?" "I'd say you are definitely in the running." "Mamie, are you telling me that I have some competition?" "Unfortunately, he's the man who owns the place where she works, the Janex Corporation. He is pushing her pretty hard. His name is Sterling something. He wanted her to go to dinner with him. "Is that right?" "He had been getting her flowers and taking her to lunch every day. Sam told me that he told her just how he felt about her before he went out of town. Bear I do know that she told him that she would think about it. "

"I guess I'd better make my move huh

Mamie?" "Well I wouldn't let any grass grow under my feet if I were you. I know she enjoys his company and he makes her laugh. It has been a long time since I have seen my baby laugh." "Where's Sam now?" "She went out to the stable to get Jake to saddle up Star and Malabar, the buckskin for you to ride. Sam thought the two of you could ride up to the lake."

Mamie told Bear, "Sam had lost someone very close to her a couple of years ago. Jimmy. They were supposed to be married in the spring but he didn't live that long. He had a heart attack and didn't make it. He was so young. No one knows what caused it or what brought it on. Sam took it hard. It has just been the last year that she has been able to let go and get on with her life." "Mamie I'll take good care of her. I know you will Bear. No one will ever hurt her as long as I'm around. I'll make her laugh too." Sam came in from the stable. "Hi Bear." "Hi Sam,Mamie told me that she has our lunch all packed." Bear, if it is alright with you I thought we could ride up to the lake and have our picnic there." "Ok Stuff?" "It has been a long time since I've had a picnic lunch Bear." "Then it is high time you did. "Would you like to ride up to the lake on horseback or take the horses with us and ride after we get up there?"

The Emerald Ring

"Let's go riding after we get up there." "Ok Bear. Here are the keys to the garage. Would you go up there and get the jeep and meet me at the stable. We'll hook up the horse trailer and then we can load up the horses." "Ok Stuff".

Bear unlocked the garage and was speechless with the collection of cars Sam had in her garage. There was a 5th Avenue, 64 Mustang convertible, a Nissan 300 SL turbo, a motor cycle, 57 T-Bird, 79 T-Bird and the jeep. Bear got the jeep and locked the garage back up. He drove the jeep to the stable where Sam was waiting for him. "Sam you sure have quite a collection of cars. Are they all yours?" "They are now. My Grandfather left them to me when he died." "Sam I sure do love your place." "Thanks Bear, Grandfather sure was proud of it. He loved it so much that it became a part of him. He will always live on this ranch. He will always be here."

Bear offered to drive the jeep and Sam agreed. "Bear have you always lived in this area?" "No, I haven't". I've been around here about five years now." "Do you like it here? I really enjoy my work here as a detective. Where are you from?" "Oklahoma." "Oklahoma, how did you end up here?"

"A friend of mine was on the police force here and needed some help so I volunteered. It had them stumped for months. We solved the case and they offered me a job and I stayed on." "What did you do in Oklahoma?" I have a horse ranch there." "You do? How many acres do you have?" "I guess it is about 1,500 acres or so. Oh my goodness. That's quite a horse ranch. My Uncle is taking care of it for me. It helps us both out. It gives him something to do and allows me to do something I really enjoy." "I see."

"Here we are Bear. Pull up over there." "Ok." Bear got the horses out of the horse trailer. They got on the horses and rode around for awhile. Sam pointed out all of her favorite places. They rode over to a bunch of big rocks and Sam sat on one with the lake at her back. Bear walked over to her and said, "Sam there is something I've got to say to you and I hope you will let me say it and not interrupt me until I'm done." "Ok Bear you sound so serious." "I am." "You are so beautiful sitting there." "Thanks Bear that means a lot to me." It does?" "Of course it does." "Then what I'm about to say will be a lot easier." Sam smiled and looked at Bear with a twinkle in her eyes. "I don't know if you know it or not but I think an awful lot of you. I think I fell in love with you the first time I saw you at the Silver Bullet." "You did?" "Why have you waited until now to tell me?" "I've seen how selective you were with your friends at the Silver Bullet and I didn't want to get started off on the wrong foot." "I see." "Mamie told me that a man named Sterling is also interested in you. So Sam do I have a chance?" "Oh Bear, I'd say you have a very good chance." While gazing into each other's eyes the heat of their passion took over. Bear took her into his arms and kissed her very passionately and held her. They pledged their love to each other and then if by magic their love was sealed as they held each other tenderly gazing across the view of the ranch. "Promise me something Bear." "Ok, what is it?" "Don't ever let anything happen to you." "I'll do you one better, I am not going to let anything happen to either one of us. We have a whole life time ahead of us. "

Chapter 9: The Zoo

"Bear I have to go to the zoo today. Would you like to go with me?" "Why are you going to the zoo?" "Once a month I take Baby there to visit a friend of hers." "Well I'll be. I think I've heard of everything now." "The Veterinarian, Jim set it up for me. He thought it would be good for her." "I agree, I'm just surprised that the Zoo lets you do it. They know Baby is in top notch shape because Jim also works at the zoo." "I see. Lucky for Baby." Sure, when do you want to go?" "After we finish eating why don't we go back to the house, pick up Baby and head for the Zoo." "I've never been to the Zoo here. This should be fun and interesting to say the least." After Sam and Bear finished eating they loaded up the horses and headed back to the house. The ride back to the house was a lot quieter. Sam nuzzled up into Bears arm that he had wrapped around her. Sam was praying quietly to herself, asking *God to please watch over them and thanking God for bringing Bear into her life.* Sam wasn't the only one praying. Bear was praying asking *God to help him take care of her and to help him make her happy.* Bear is so happy he can't believe that Sam is finally his. When they arrived home they went in to get Baby. Baby heard Sam coming down the hall and was waiting for Sam when she came into the bedroom. Sam wrestled with her a little bit and asked her if she was ready to go and visit her friend at the Zoo. Bear joined Sam and Baby on the floor. Sam slipped away and called the Zoo while Bear was playing with her so Jim knew they were on the way. Sam picked up Baby's collar off the dresser and Baby got all excited. Baby knew when she put on the collar she was going to get to go somewhere. "Wait a minute Baby. Don't get so excited. I can't get your collar on. Baby calmed down and Sam slipped on her collar. Off they went to the jeep.

Sam saw Frank and asked him to put the horses away for her. then she walked over to Star and kissed him on the nose. She patted him on the head and told him she would see him later. "I love you Star."

Mamie and Shamrock saw Bear and Sam with Baby in the jeep and went outside. "Hi Mamie, Shamrock, everything ok?" "Great!" "I went fishing this morning and caught a mess of fish. Mamie cooked them up for me for lunch." "Mamie, Bear and I are taking Baby to the Zoo for her monthly visit. I doubt we will be back for supper." While Sam was telling Mamie and

Shamrock, Bear was behind her giving the ok sign.

Mamie and Shamrock started giggling. "What's so funny?" "Nothing Sam." Sam turns around and asks Bear, "What are you doing?" "I'm not doing anything." Mamie told them to have a good time. Sam called Mamie over to the side. "Mamie, Bear told me that he is in love with me." "Oh sweetheart, I'm so happy for you. What did you say to him?" Mamie was crossing her fingers and holding her breath. "Well, I told him I was in love with him too." "O' praise the Lord." While Sam was confiding in Mamie, Bear was bending Shamrocks ear. "Shamrock, she loves me." "That's great Bear. I wouldn't let my guard down though. There is a man named Sterling that is just as much in love with her as he is. Bear I don't think that he is going to give up on her." "Is that right?" Sam hopped into the jeep with Baby and Bear. "Baby seems to have taken a liken to you Bear." Baby was trying to sit in Bears lap. Sam scratched Baby's ears and gave her a pet trying to get her to sit down. "What am I going to do with you Sam?" "I don't know. I can't believe I fell in love with a woman who has a cougar, horses, birds and all those other critters." "No one else would love them like I do. Each one is very special to me." "You're probably right." Bear started the jeep and they were off to the Zoo.

Bear and Sam finally arrives at the Zoo with Baby. Sam showed Bear the employee entrance to go through and they headed for the Managers office where Jim was waiting for them. Bear beeped the horn and Jim came out of the office. "Jim I'd like you to meet Bear. Bear is a very special friend of mine. Bear this is Jim. Jim's been a good friend of mine for many years and I wouldn't trust any of my animals with anyone else. I love him dearly." "Sam, do I need to be jealous of Jim." Jim laughed and said, "No you don't have to worry about me. Sam and I are like brother and sister. We do love each other alright but nothing ever developed between us. We joke about it sometimes and wonder how two people who love each other so much doesn't have a physical relationship, but oh well, that is just the way it is." Bear replied, "Lucky for me." Jim jumped into the jeep and they headed for the Cougar area. Sam gave Baby a big hug and Bear told her to be a good girl. Jim took the leash off and lead Baby to her playmates door and Baby went right in. They started playing right away.

"They sure do make a cute pair." "They

sure do and one of these days when I come to bring her home I'm going to end up with a bunch of cubs on my hands."

Bear told Sam, "You'll love it." "Oh I know." Jim added. The Zoo keeps telling her if that happens she can leave the cubs at the Zoo and they will take care of them. Little did Baby know that this stay was going to be a lot longer than the other visits.

Jim handed Bear the VIP pass and told them to enjoy the rest of the afternoon on him. Sam looked at Bear and they thanked him, then they headed out to enjoy the Zoo. First stop was the bird house. Bear looked at Sam while she was looking at all the birds. "Bear look at all the beautiful birds." He sees a twinkle in her eye as she gazes from one to the other. "I know Sam; you wish you could take all of them home with you." "Yeah, wouldn't that be something." "What's next?" "I think the monkey house is next." "Ok let's go." "I see it over there, hurry." "Ok Sam." Sam and Bear watched the monkeys for awhile and laughed until it hurt. "Sam I think we had better start thinking about supper."

Would you like to go out somewhere and eat?" "That would be nice Bear." "Where would you like to go?" "I don't care, surprise me."

The Emerald Ring

Bear thought to himself, S*urprise her, I bet that Sterling fella has taken her to every nice place in town. Where am I going to take her?* Ok Sam. Sam and Bear started heading back to the jeep. *I guess I could take her to Tony's. He has a special place set up in back just for his special customers and friends for that special night out. It even has a patio and a view.*

On the way to the restaurant Sam is thinking. *How am I going to tell Sterling that I've committed myself to someone now? It's not going to be easy. I really like Sterling. I hope we will be able to stay close friends. I told him that I didn't have anyone in my life right now and now I am going to tell him that I am taken. I know he's going to be hurt. I just hope he will understand.*

Bear pulled up to the restaurant and parked the jeep." Here we are Sam. I hope you like it." Bear walked over to open the jeep door for her. Sam smiled." A very close friend of mine owns it." When Sam and Bear walked in Tony noticed Bear right away and went over to greet them. "Bear, I'm so happy to see you. What can I do for you? Bear for you everything is on the house." "Tony I would like to introduce you to my girl, Sam. Sam this is a very good friend of mine Tony." "Tonight I am going to make you a very special dinner just for you."

Tony took them to the back of the restaurant. Bear was watching Sam to see her reaction hoping that she would like it. He could tell by the look on her face that she was pleased. Bear was thinking to himself *Stuff that in your hat Sterling.*

Everything looks so romantic. Candles on the table and soft music, Bear had never taken anyone to this part of the restaurant before and he even had to admit even he was impressed. He knew the food was good because his friend had won several cooking contests. Tony brought a special wine to their table. "Bear, this is a wonderful place, however did you find it?" "Tony found me. That's a long story." The setting was breathtaking. There was a walk over bridge going across a large fish pond. A waterfall flowed into the fish pond and beautiful flowers with shrubs all around it. This was a special night so Tony catered to them personally.

Tony started them off with a salad with his famous salad dressing. Next he brought them a bowl of fresh ham and bean soup with hot homemade rolls. Sam and Bear didn't talk much while they were eating. Tony was busting with pride. He could tell they really liked his food. Tony also noticed the aura of love that surrounded them. There was no doubt about it these two were definitely in love. It brought such joy to Tony's heart to see Bear in love. Tony was a romantic at heart anyway.

Even though not much was spoken, Sam and Bear looked into each others eyes and their thoughts were exchanged. Sammy's shy little girl grin would show and Bears eyes danced with excitement with being in love. After they had finished their soup Tony brought them the most tender, juicy filet mignon he could find. Char broiled over a flame to a medium pink on the inside. Tony marinated them the night before giving them a special taste you could only get at Tony's.

With the steak he also served them a steamy hot baked potato with butter and sour cream. Fresh green beans cooked with new potatoes and ham, seasoned to perfection. A side dish of cottage cheese. A fresh baked loaf of bread. Definitely a meal fit for a King.

When they finished eating Bear walked Sam over to the waterfall. "This is a wonderful place Bear." "I was hoping that you would like it. I didn't know where to take you." "It's perfect." There was music playing in the background, Tony saw to that. The music in the background was My Endless Love. Bear looked into Sammy's eyes and said, "Sam I know I haven't known you very long but I think you know how much you mean to me. I would like the chance to show you if you would let me. I love you Sam and I would like you to become my wife. You would make me the happiest man in the World." Sam looked into Bears eyes, paused for a minute, and said, "Yes Bear I will. I'd be honored to become your wife." "Oh Sam if you only knew how happy you have just made me."

Bear motioned for Tony to come over. He was so excited that he just had to tell someone. "Tony, this beautiful lady has just consented to become my wife." Tony shook Bears hand and then gave him a hug. "Congratulations!" Tony gave Sam a hug and a kiss. "I am so happy for the both of you." Tony ordered a bottle of Champagne. They all three toasted the occasion. Then Tony left the happy couple alone.

Standing in front of the beautiful waterfall Bear took Sammy into his arms and held her ever so gently. "Bear I wish this moment could last forever." "It will last forever Sammy. It will be in our hearts for always. No one can ever take away our memories or our dreams." "I

The Emerald Ring

can't wait until Mamie and Shamrock find out
that we are getting married. Bear laughed and
told Sam, "I bet they try to put us in the car and
take us to the Judge to marry us right away so
we can't change our minds." Sam joined Bear
in the laughter and agreed. Bear looked at
Sam and asked "If you don't mind Sam, I would
like to have a special ceremony. This is a
special moment in our life and I want it to be
perfect." "That's fine with me. Whatever you
want." "I've waited a long time for this day. I
know that the wedding is supposed to be for
the bride, but now a day's brides are doing
strange things for weddings." "I understand
Bear and I feel the same way." "Thanks Sam."

Chapter 10: The Narrow Escape

Just then they noticed Steve from the Police Department. "I wonder what he is doing here." Steve noticed them right away and headed for them. "Bill told me that I might find you hear Bear." "What is going on?" Bear asked Steve. "You know the fire at the Janex Corporation?" Yes." "Well we found out that it wasn't an accident. We are pretty sure we know who set it." "That right?" "All of our evidence points to the Supervisor at the dock and one other man who works in the Administration office." "Not Mr. McFadden", Sam asked? "No a guy by the name of Pete. He is the Vice President." "I haven't seen much of him." Steve told them that he had been watching him for a long time. "This was the first time I've been able to get anything on him concrete enough to lock him up. Sam started telling Steve what she found out and hoped it was enough on him to close him down. "Well maybe with what we both have we can lock him up for a long time." Steve told them that they had better be careful because if they suspect that you have anything on them you might not live long enough to tell anyone about it. "Great, I ask a girl to marry me and you bring in tidings of doom." "I'm sorry Bear. Congratulations!"

"Well guys don't look now but we may be in trouble." Steve and Bear turned around just in time to see Jack Anderson and Pete Haley heading straight for them. Bear signals Tony and a couple of his boys to detain them while they go out the back door. "I've got a feeling that they know we are on to them." Bear agreed and told Sam that he had never seen them in there before. "I guess if they come through that door then we know that they are not here for the food. I don't think that it is just a coincidence. They know we know so we had better be careful. They will try to kill us before we can get all the evidence together for an arrest. If we arrest them now they will get out on bond and we won't accomplish anything. Look out! There they are." "They've got guns." Let's get out of here." Steve takes off. Bear and Sam jumped into the jeep and took off. They followed Bear and Sam instead of Steve. Bear told Sam "We can't go back to the ranch it's too dangerous. Bear called Mamie on the phone in the jeep. Mamie told Shamrock that the jeep is on the corner of Forest and Robin Hood by the railroad tracks. "Don't have time to explain now Mamie but tell Shamrock to be very careful. They may be watching the jeep. Sam and I will call you later. The keys are under the left fender."

"Sam I'm sorry but we are going to have to catch that train." "Are you serious?" "Look out, there they are." Sam and Bear jumped onto the boxcar just as they started shooting at them. By the time the two men had reached the train, the speed had picked up to where they couldn't jump on. "Now what Bear?" "I don't know yet, but I will think of something." Bear told Sam to think of this as an adventure. "Great! Like I don't get enough adventure in my life as it is." "First thing we have to do is find out where this train is heading. Ok?" That was the first thing that they were going to do. "Then we have to figure out how to lose them. I've got a feeling that we're not dealing with amateurs here. It's not going to be easy to lose them. I don't think they are going to give up until they see us laying lifeless somewhere." I think you're right Bear." "You know when I got involved with this I never dreamed that it would ever get this dangerous. I've been in sticky situations before so I guess we can get out of this one." "That's my girl. There should be a town not too far from here if the train starts slowing down enough we can jump off." Listen." What?" "Do you hear that?" "What?" "Hear it?" "Yeah, it's a whistle."

The Emerald Ring

"Great Sam, that means that the train is going to slow down. Let's get ready to jump. Ok . Jump Sam."

Bear and Sam jumped off the train and rolled down the embankment. "Are you ok Sam?" "Yes, I'm fine." You ok?" "I'm ok."

"We're going to have to find a place to get a couple of hours sleep. There's a farmhouse over there Bear." "Maybe we can sleep in the barn." "Maybe." "In the morning let's find a phone and call Mamie and Shamrock." "We don't have to wait until morning Bear. We can call her from here." "How?" "My phone, I took it out of the jeep and put it in my pocket when I saw we were in trouble." "Sam, you are amazing." After they climbed the fence and crossed a field they finally make it to the barn. Luckily Sam and Bear both had a re-pore with animals. Making their way to the hayloft the animals didn't make a sound. It was like the animals sensed that Sam and Bear were in trouble and needed help. Bear fluffed up some hay in the loft. They called home to check in and to let them know that they were ok and also to let them know what was going on. "Hello Mamie." "Hello Sam are you guys alright?" "We're fine." "Tell Bear... just a minute, you tell Bear." "Bear, the friend of yours at the

Police Department, Steve." Yes." "He came by here and asked if we had heard from you yet. He had been shot." "Is he going to be alright?" "Yes, he will be ok. He said those two men took off and chased you instead of him so he turned around to follow them. He figured that you might need some help. He saw you get on the train and knew you were safe. He was turning around when they saw him and they got him in the shoulder. He was able to lose them. Then he saw Shamrock and he brought him out here. "Where is he now?" "He had another officer come out here and take him to the hospital. He said after the hospital fixes him up he has a friend that he can go stay with. He knew he would be safe there." Good. We'll check back with you later Shamrock."

The doors were open in the hayloft so they could see for miles. Before lying down to sleep they looked out across the country side and marveled at how beautiful everything looked under a full moon. Everything seemed so peaceful at that moment. They thanked God for keeping them safe.

"Well Sam we had better bunk down and try to get some sleep. We have a lot to do tomorrow." "How long do you think we are going to have to hide out?" "I don't know but I

The Emerald Ring

hope it is not for long. No telling what tomorrow holds for us. Let's get some sleep. I don't want you to worry Sam. I won't let anything happen to you. In the morning I'll find out where we are and get a hold of some friends of mine and they will help us. Bear laid down and Sam snuggled up in Bears arms. Bear gave Sam a kiss on the forehead and they fell asleep. They must have been exhausted because they slept all through the night. It seemed like they had just closed their eyes when they heard the rooster crow. "Sam doesn't it seem like we just laid down." I know, huh. We had better get going."

Sam and Bear made their way to the highway. "Look there is a sign. Clarksville three miles." "Bear I know someone in Clarksville." "You do?" "Yeah, Granny." "Who's Granny?" "I've known her all my life. Everyone just loves her. We just kind of adopted her. She's quite a character. Did you ever watch the Beverly Hillbillies? Remember Granny, well that's kind of what Granny is like." "Ok, do you think she will help us?" "Are you kidding? If they catch up to us she'll have lots of fun with them." "She sounds like my kind of lady." "You'll like her alright. Well let's get going." When they reach town Sam told Bear that she was hungry. "Ok Sam, We'll find a restaurant and give Granny a call." "Thanks Bear." "We need to keep a low profile in case they come looking for us. We don't want to give them any leads." "There's Ginny's. Let's eat there. I've heard Granny talk about this place. A friend of hers owns it." Great!" "Let's go." "I'm hungry Bear. There's Ginny." They walked over and introduced themselves to her. "Well Sammy I just can't believe it. You're all growed up. Let me look at you." Does Granny know that you are here?" "No not yet." "Tell you what. Why don't you kids go upstairs and get cleaned up and I'll fix you something to eat. I'll give Granny a call for you." "Thanks. That sounds wonderful Ginny. We really appreciate it." Go on." Ginny orders up a big country breakfast for them and then called Granny. "Hi Granny, how you doing?" "What's up Ginny?" Granny knew something was up right away. She could tell by the sound of her voice. They knew each other to well. "Sam is here Granny and I think she is in some kind of trouble. Sam has a gentleman friend with her." Granny shouts, "Hallelujah, my prayers have been answered." "Sam wanted me to call you." "Tell them I'll be thar as fast as I can git thar. If my little girl needs me then she knows she can count on me. What's the fella like?" "He's a well built handsome dude. He'd make quite a catch Granny.""Better tell her to hang on to this guy." "I sense that they are running from someone. I don't think the guy she is with though would run from anyone or anything." "You don't say." Sam wouldn't back down from anybody either." "This sounds serious. Sounds like they need Granny alright. I'm on my way."

While Granny was getting dressed and ready to go, Ginny took up their breakfast. "Here you go. Granny told me to tell you that she is on her way." Bear looks at the breakfast then looks at Ginny. "Ginny you're an Angel!" "Well Bear I've been called a lot of things but an Angel was not one of them." All of a sudden they heard a screeching sound. "That will be Granny." "Granny?" "Yes Granny." "Granny drives like that?" "Well, you see Granny does just about whatever Granny wants. She has her own way of looking at things and if her mind is made up then that is the way it is. There is no way of changing her mind. She is a real tough cookie."

All of a sudden the door opened up. There stood Granny, a whole five feet. She had on old tennis shoes, jeans, and a long over shirt that hung down over her jeans. Her hair was all a mess. Not to her of course. She didn't have any teeth but you could see her smile as she drew her mouth to one side and would give a wink of her eye. That is how you could tell she was in a good mood. "Sammy come here girl. Let me look at you. Boy, you sure have growed. Now sit yourself down and tell Granny all about it." "About what Granny?" "Come on Sammy this is Granny you're talking to." Ok Granny but it's a long story." "I've got all the time in the world child. First tell me who this good looking gent is." "Granny, this is Bear."

"Bear are you taking good care of my little girl?" "I'm trying to Mam." "Don't call me Mam. You can call me Granny, everybody else does." "Granny, Bear and I are getting married." "Oh hallelujah. Bear, I'm right happy to meet you. I was starting to worry about you Sam. Having a fella in your life makes it all worthwhile. Now tell me, what can ole Granny do for you?" "You see Granny there are two guys that are trying to kill us. We have the evidence that can lock them up for a long time. Bear is a police detective but we can't arrest them yet. We have to get all the evidence collected on them otherwise they may get away with just a fine and still try to find us and that wouldn't do any good. "

They finish up their breakfast and Sam told Ginny that she needed to call Mamie and

The Emerald Ring

Shamrock to see if they were ok. "Sure Sam. Go ahead." Sam called Mamie and as soon as she heard Sam's voice she was relieved. "Sam, how are you and Bear?" "We're fine Mamie. Was Shamrock able to get my jeep alright?" "Yes, it is already back in the garage and he was sure that nobody saw him. He was real careful." "I'm at Ginny's now Mamie with Granny and as soon as I find out anything else I will let you know." Shamrock came into the kitchen with Mamie and she told him that she had Sam on the phone. "Shamrock wants to talk to Bear." "Bear I didn't want to worry Mamie but your buddy on the Police Department has been killed. Someone slipped into the hospital and when no one was looking they shot him." "I think I'll take Sam to my ranch in Oklahoma. We should be safe there for awhile. You have the number there in case you need to get a hold of us. Meanwhile I will keep you informed of where we are." "Ok Bear, talk to you later." "Wait Shamrock, I have something else to tell you." "What?" "I asked Sam to marry me and she said yes. Tell Mamie for us ok? Shamrock, you take good care of Mamie for me; don't let anything happen to her." "I'll take good care of her Bear. I think she is pretty special myself. You guys be careful." "We will."

There is a knock at the door. It was the waitress. "Ginny there are two men down stairs asking about those two people." Granny jumps in, "I'll take care of this." She headed down stairs. "Something I can do for you boys?" We're looking for two people and were wondering if you might have seen them." The men gave Granny a description of Bear and Sam. Granny starts questioning them. "Nope I ain't seen anyone like that."

"We are with an insurance company and we are trying to settle a claim, that's all." I see. No reward huh?" "Well if you see them and you call us we might be able to work out something." "Well I ain't seen them but if I do what number do I call to reach you?" The men gave her a number to call or leave a message. "I'll keep a look out boys but nothing exciting ever happens in this town." "Thanks Mam. Good day to you." The two men headed out the door. Granny headed out the door a few minutes after them.

Granny went over to her jeep and pulled out her shotgun and aimed it at their car when Bear stopped her just in time. "Granny what are you doing?" "I'm gittin' rid of those two varmints. You see that way we don't have to worry about um. No one is going to mess with my little girl. I won't have it." "It's ok Granny nothing is going to happen to her. I need to get us some transportation Granny. Do you have any ideas?" "Well let's go back upstairs."

Bear told Sam and Ginny that they were right about Granny. She is a sly ole fox. "Sam, she was getting ready to shoot them with a shotgun." "Yep, that sounds like Granny." "What were you thinking Granny? The police would have locked you up for killing them. No, I don't think so. Ed wouldn't lock me up for killing those two varmints." "You know she is probably right." "So much for that, you two need some transportation. If you take me to a dealership Granny, I can get us something." "Sure Sonny, Let's go. Maybe we'll run into those two guys again and I can git another whack at um." "Granny you have to promise me something." "Sure Sonny, what?" "You have to promise to let Sam and I handle this. We don't need you knocking someone off just because you think it is the right thing to do." "I can't do that Sonny but I can promise you that I won't go looking for um. As long as they stay out of my way I'll leave them alone. Deal?" "Deal."

"Here we are Bear, Fred's used car lot. You go pick out something and I'll go talk to Fred." "Ok Granny." "You know Fred is kind of sweet on me, the old buzzard." Somehow I got the feeling she liked the old coot even though she pretended she didn't. I could tell by the way she waddled over to him. Bear looked over the lot and picked out a four wheel drive. It was just what they needed. Bear walked up to Fred and Granny. Granny asked Bear if he found anything. "I think that four wheel drive will do just fine." "Bear what was the price on the windshield? $3,500.00 dollars." "Ok Fred we will give you $2,000.00. Final no haggling." "I can't do that." "Ok then bye."

Bear and Granny started heading for the jeep. "Wait, wait I'm sure we can work out something." "I told you Fred $2,000.00 and that's it." "Ok you got yourself a deal."

Bear and Granny headed for the office to sign the paperwork. "Fred, there had better not be anything wrong with this machine or I'll be back." "It's ok Granny, you can trust me." "Yeah right."

Bear and Granny headed back to Ginny's. Bear motioned Granny to pull over to the gas station so he could fill up the tank. He picked up a map while he was there. "Hey Sonny, thar's a CB in thar. Do you know how to use it?" Sure do Mam. I mean Granny." "If you git out thar and need me give me a holler,

The Emerald Ring

Everyone knows how to git hold of me."
"Thanks Granny."

    Meanwhile Sam was packing up some
food for them to take along. Sam knew that the
next couple of days were uncertain. Ginny
gave her a couple of blankets. Ginny told Sam
that she sure has a handsome guy. "He's
wonderful Ginny." "I think Granny likes him. You
know Granny Sam. She would not have offered
to help him if she didn't." "I know she is quite a
character alright." Sam and Ginny heard a
screech. Granny and Bear are back. A few
minutes later Bear and Granny came through
the door. Granny asks Sam, "Everything ok?"
"Everything is fine here, how did you two do?"
"Bear found him a four wheel drive. A
Renegade and it's a nice looking machine. You
kids want me to go with you?" "No Granny we'll
be ok. I can take care of myself and besides
that I have Bear to take care of me now." "Well,
that is yet to be seen." "Granny!" "Ok I'll be
nice." Sam walked over to the window and
looked down the street to see what Bear had
picked up for their journey. "I love it. It's great,
we can go anywhere in it." "Yep, and thar's a
CB in thar and your fella told me he knowed
how to use it. So if you git into trouble use it.
I'll git there as quick as I kin."

129

Janet McBaine

Sam told Bear about the food they packed up and Ginny gave us a few blankets to take along. Bear walked over to Ginny and gave her a big bear hug. "Thanks Ginny for all you help. We really do appreciate it." Then Granny bellows out, "How come I didn't git a hug?" Bear broke out into laughter. Granny says, "What's everybody laughing about?" "Come here Granny." Bear gave her a big bear hug and kissed her on the forehead. Granny's face turned red and you could see the half cocked smile and the twinkle in her eye as she looked down to the floor.

"Granny, I've never seen you blush before. I knew there was a softy underneath that rough exterior of yours. Come on now let's get this stuff loaded up." "Good idea. You never know when we might have to take off in a hurry." After loading the jeep, Sam, Bear and Granny looked over the map to plan a route.

There is a knock at the door. Ginny opened the door and it was the waitress. "I hate to bother you, but the two men that were here earlier are back again." "Let me at um", Granny says. "I know Granny. I know, but wait a minute, let's use this to our advantage." "Good thinking Sonny." "Granny I wish you would quit calling me Sonny, I really don't like that." "Ok

The Emerald Ring

Bear." "that's better." "Why don't I go down and keep them company for awhile and you two slip down the back stairs and git away." "Good thinking Granny." Bear looked at her. "Don't worry Sonny, I mean Bear. I won't do anything that's not called for." "I'm proud of you Granny." Bear gave her another big hug. Sam and Bear went down the stairs while Granny made her entrance into the restaurant.

"Well looky here. It's those two good looking guys from this morning. Kinda miss me did ya? If you guys are nice, I'll let you buy me dinner, how about it boys?" "Well, uh, ok Mam. "Are you going to be here long?" "No, we're leaving after we eat." "Shame, I thought you boys might want to take a good looker like me dancing."

Sam and Bear got into the jeep and took off. About ten minutes later a man came into the restaurant looking for the men looking for Bear and Sam. He spotted them over at the table with Granny. The man asked, "Are you the two men looking for the man and woman?" "Yes, yes we are. Did you see them?" "Yes I did. I saw them heading out of town about ten minutes ago." "The two men started to head out of the restaurant when the waitress and Granny stopped them. "Hey, you can't leave without paying your bill." "Ok, ok. Ray, you go pay the bill and I'll go and check in with the boss." Granny slipped out and lets the air out of their tires, then slipped back in and started eating. "I really appreciate you guys buying me dinner. Wish you could stick around with me and help me eat it. You could keep me company." "Sorry Mam something has come up and we really have to go." Ray hung up the phone and they hurried out to their car.

Hurriedly they jump into their car and start to back up when they realize that they had flat tires. They hurry back into the restaurant and try to find someone to fix their flat tires. Granny sees them come back into the restaurant and in a loud voice says, "I knew you boys didn't want to leave me. I knew you would be back." "Shut up lady and leave us alone." "Well you don't have to be nasty about it." "Sorry lady but we are busy right now." Not able to find anyone to fix their tires they started asking where the nearest gas station is. It is a couple of miles down the road. Granny offered to call the station since she knew the owner, Bill. Granny told the boys, "No problem he is a friend of mine." Granny called him alright. She told him to take at least two or three hours or longer if he wanted. "Ok Granny, anything for you." Granny told the boys that he was sending someone over to fix the tires right away. "Why don't you boys come on over and finish eating." "Ok, ok lady. We might as well."

Meanwhile Sam and Bear were quite a few miles down the road. "I think we will head for my ranch in Oklahoma if that is ok with you. We'll be safe there." "Ok." "I hope you like it Sam." If it has horses on it you know I'll love it." "No problem there." "Ok. How many horses do you have?" "Hard telling, what do you mean?" "Well you'll see...

All of a sudden they hear Granny on the CB. "You kids got your ears on? This is Grannyjammer here. All you truckers out thar, they're heading West. Watch out for my babies. They're driving a four wheel drive black Renegade. Got your ears on Bear?" "Got um on Granny." "Those two varmints left here twenty minutes ago. I figure you should have a couple of hours on them. You trucker buddies out there be watching for a brown Chevy, car license number SLR251. Those fella's are trying to hurt my babies. Bear talk to me. You got a handle these truckers can communicate with you on?" "Sure do Grannyjammer, its Big Mac." "That figures." "Hey Big Mac is that you? This is Buzzardbait." "Hey I haven't heard from you in a while, where have you been?" "Catch you up on that later; I've got a pressing problem right now." "Hear you loud and clear."

"This is wrong number Big Mac. Grannyjammer just filled me in." "We've got you covered Big Mac. Just keep your peddle to the metal and we'll do the rest. Winemaker to Big Mac, This car you're scooten from is on my back door." "I copy that Winemaker." "Big Mac, This is Under Cover Lover at you." "I've got you guys at my front door. Let's play some hide and seek."

"This is Boogie Woogie, I'm in, 10-4" "Rhythm Maker here at your front door count me in partner, 10-4 Winemaker to Big Mac." "I just passed Lil's Truck Stop. He's still at my back door. 10-4 partner." "Rhythm Maker to Big Mac looks like a storm coming in." "I copy that partner we've been watching it." "Hey you guys with your ears on Big Mac pulling over to get some gas. We just passed the 157 marker." "Catch you later Big Mac."

Bear pulled over, fills up the tank and checked the oil and water. Sam went into the ladies room and freshened up for a minute. "You ready Stuff?" "Ready." "I got us a soda." "Thanks Bear. What are you going to do if they catch up to us?" "Don't worry. We have the best protection you could ask for. Truckers.

The Emerald Ring

We'll be ok, don't worry."

Back on the road again, Bear checked in with the truckers. The sun was setting and it had started to rain pretty hard. The wind had also picked up so driving had become a problem. The shadows of cars soon became lights in the distance. By now Bear had caught up with Buzzardbait and Wrong Number. "Hey you partners out there, we'd better pull over. There's a man up ahead swinging a lantern back and forth like he wants us to stop." "10-4 partner. We're right behind you." Bear, Wrong Number and Buzzard Bait walked down the road trying to find the man with the lantern." I know I saw him. Something must have happened to him." Here, come here." "I found the lantern." "Where is the man that was swinging the lantern?" "Let's see if we can find him. Something must have happened to him." The men looked all around but couldn't find him. They walked down the road a little ways and found that the road had been washed out. If they hadn't stopped they would have driven off into the raven and been killed. They all agreed that something strange was going on. When the men got back to their trucks they notified the police that the bridge was out. The police thanked them. Immediately they blocked off the road so the public would be able to detour. Luckily they were able to report the bridge out before there were any fatalities. The police told them not to worry about the man with the lantern. "Why's that?" "Every now and then during a storm we get the same story." I checked into it and found that a truck driver some years back had wrecked in a storm and was killed. Some people believe that he comes back to warn people in danger. They all looked at each other and walked back to their trucks.

"Well partners I'd really like to stick around and visit but we're going to have to get out of here. "Sure thing Big Mac." "We got you covered. Sam and Bear took off not knowing what to do next; just knowing that time was very important. The storm was starting to let up a little now. They would just have to come back after their car later. They packed what they could carry and made their way down the bank to a place where they could get across. Wrong Number radioed Granny and she caught a ride up to their Renegade and took it back to her place. She knew Bear would keep on going and not back track as long as those guys were after them.

Sam started sneezing and Bear came running over to her. "Sam, I think you're coming down with something. I had better get you in somewhere I can get you warm." "Bear don't worry, I'll be fine." "Of course you will but I think we'd better find a place for the night anyway." They found a cave with a lot of room in it. "This is perfect Bear. I love it. It's nice and cozy and no one will find us in here." Bear looked around and found some dry firewood, then built a fire so Sam could get warm. Luckily they had grabbed their back packs when they took off walking. Bear also grabbed the food and blankets and hung them up to dry. The heat from the fire would dry them in no time at all. While the blankets were drying Bear gathered some greener branches so he could make a pallet for them by placing a blanket over them.

While they sat next to the fire Sam fixed them some of the food Ginny had sent along with them. They ate a little bit and then Bear threw the blanket over the branches. Sam laid down with Bear next to her. He watched her through the night making sure she was going to be alright. A couple of hours before sun up he caught a few hours of sleep. Bear woke up before Sam so he went exploring to see what he could find to eat. He brought back some berries and some apples. He picked some wild flowers on the way back for Sam. He found some large rocks and he placed them in a circle inside the fire in the cave. The rocks would help keep them warm after the fire would go out. Bear found a big branch and tied some smaller ones on it with a vine to sweep out the cave a little. He found some gourds and he hollowed them out to use to drink out of.

Sam was still sleeping so he looked through the back pack again to see what they had to work with. He found some string. He remembered seeing a bee hive by the place where he found the berries. Bear left again and found the bee hive. Bear knocked down the bee hive and the bees swarmed all around.

Bear stayed hidden until the bees left. He separated the honey from the wax. He found a long straight stick and stuck it into the ground several times. He cut the string in several places and placed the string into the hole until a little bit was above the ground. He then heated up the wax and poured it into the holes. He let the wax cool and loosened up the dirt around the wax. Now they would have some candles. He went back into the cave and found Sam still sleeping. The canteens were full of water and they had fruit and berries to eat. Bear laid down next to Sam and slept until she woke up.

When Sam woke up and saw what Bear

had done while she was sleeping she was amazed. All of a sudden she started crying. Bear heard her crying and woke up. "What's wrong Sam? Are you ok?" "Yes Bear, I'm just fine. I just found the flowers you picked for me. That was so sweet of you. I just started crying. I'm so happy. You're amazing. How could anyone not love you?" Well you're a pretty special lady yourself." Sam blushed. "Breakfast! What do you mean breakfast?" "I found some fruit and berries so I thought we could have them for breakfast." "Oh thank you Bear!" After eating they decided to look around and see what was in the area around them.

They found a place where Bear could catch some fish for them to eat. "Well Bear, looks like things are looking up. We have fish fruit and berries to eat." "Not bad huh? I have a surprise for you." "What's that?" I know I can find something around here for you to use for tea and I found a bee hive and I have some honey you can use to sweeten your tea. Talk about a blessing. Wow! "Can we head back to the cave now and check it out?" "Sure."When they got back to the cave they started to explore it when Bear said, "Sam I can't believe it, look over there." Further back into the cave they ran across a waterfall that flowed down into the pool of water. Over to one side they found a homemade stove that someone had rigged up some time ago. "From the looks of it no one had used it for quite some time." Bear lifted up a piece of canvas and found some pots and pans. Sam shouted out "We can cook. I don't mind roughing it but even that has its limits." Bear laughed. "I guess we had better pack our stuff and get out of here." "I don't think so. We can have some fun here for a couple of days. We can even relax a little bit. I don't think anyone is going to find us in here. Let's just take a breather and enjoy the time we have here. It's not every day you find a place like this. "Ok Sam but we still have to be careful. I know Bear."

"Ok, so what do we do now?" "I don't know." Bear suggested fishing. "Good idea but how are we going to catch them?" Bear told her to leave it up to him. Bear carved a spear out of one of the branches. "Ok let's go." Sam and Bear walked along the water until Bear found the right spot. "Ok Sam, you sit over there and watch." "Ok Bear but I still don't see how you are going to catch any fish. Bear waded out into the water and stood very still. Sam sat quietly and then all of a sudden, faster than you could blink an eye, Bear speared a fish and tossed it to the bank. Sam ran over and grabbed it. Quickly Bear threw four more over to the bank.

"Do you think that will be enough?" "Sure, but how are we going to cook them?" "Leave it up to me Sam." Ok." Sam and Bear clean the fish and headed back to the cave. "Sam did you see those large leaves when we came into the cave? I want you to go and pick about a dozen of them for me. Ok?" Bear told Sam that he would be back in a minute. Bear collected some wild plants to put with the fish to help flavor them while they were cooking. He headed back to the cave.

Bear showed Sam how to build a fire in a pit and told her about the wild plants he had picked. They wrapped the fish in the large leaves with the other wild plants that he had picked. They placed the fish in the pit and covered them up. "Ok now what?" "That's it. We can come back in an hour or so and they will be ready to eat." "Fantastic!"

"Sam, I think I spotted a corn field when I was spearing the fish." "You did?" "When did you have time to see that?" "I'm going to go and check it out. Why don't you sit here and enjoy the quiet time." Bear left and Sam checked out the pool of water. Sam's curiosity started getting the best of her and she headed for the waterfall inside the cave.

Janet McBaine

Why would someone stay in this cave? I wonder if he was hiding out from the law. Maybe he was a prospector. This waterfall is just awesome. All of a sudden Sam notices a walkway behind the waterfall. Sam was thinking to herself, *That's funny. I never noticed that before.* Sam headed toward the opening behind the waterfall and then noticed a shimmering reflection on the ceiling and walls of the cave behind the waterfall. She walked in a little further and said, "Oh my." Sam had stumbled onto a vein of gold probably worth a fortune. Sam heard Bear calling her. "I'm over here Bear." "Where?" I can hear you but I can't see you. It sounds like you are behind the waterfall." "I am." "How did you get there?" "Look over to the left of the waterfall next to the wall of the cave." "I still don't see anything." "Follow my voice." "Ok Sam." "There you are." Bear walked through. "Look at this Bear." "This is awesome." Sam noticed a large chest next to a wheel barrel. "Bear come here. Look. I wonder what is in it." "I don't know. Let's open it up and see." Sam's curiosity was getting the best of her. "Hurry Bear open it up." Bear opened up the chest and they both stood there amazed at what they had found. Huge nuggets of gold! "What are we going to do with it? We need to find out who owns this ground. Good idea. If it belongs to the farmer where we found the corn then I know he could use it." "Let's check it out. Wouldn't that be something?" "Ok but we can't do it right now. I know", said Sam.

"If this land does belong to the farmer then we have to be careful not to endanger them because of us. Those men who are chasing us are not the friendly type." "You're right. We have got to find a way to get them up here and yet not see us." "After we eat the fish we'll go down and take a look to see what we can find out. Remember Sam we can't let them see us." After eating they went out to gather up the candles. They loosened up the dirt around them and put them into their bag. "Bear, this is a terrific idea how ever did you think of it?" Bear told her, You'd be surprised at what a person can do if they put their mind to it." "I guess so." They gathered up some more fire wood for the night. "I'm having so much fun Bear." "Don't let your guard down Sam. There is one thing that I have learned that has kept me alive." "What is that?" "Don't under estimate your enemy. Always be on guard." "I know Bear. We can still have fun though can't we?" "Sure Sam I just don't want anything to happen to you."

"Bear that fish was really good. That was

fun digging it up and unwrapping it and eating it." You had some doubt?" "No." "No. You seemed surprised." "Well I guess maybe I did think a little bit that it wasn't going to be very good." "I see", said Bear. "Well, I can see right now the course I took on survival at the college must have been for city people, not for the people who are really out in the elements so to speak. "

"Are you ready to go?" Little by little they make their way to the farm house. Sam told Bear to look out, here come the kids. Bear told Sam that he saw them earlier when he was getting the corn. "Listen. Can you hear what they are saying?" "No, let's get a little closer." They moved up a little closer. The two boys were talking about what they heard their parents talking about earlier. They looked so serious and down in the dumps. I wondered why.

The two boy's names were Don and Steve. Don asked Steve, "Do you really think we're going to lose the farm?" "It sounds like it." "What are we going to do?" "I don't know." I know Mom and Dad are worried. They keep telling us that everything is going to be ok." Steve said, "I wish there was something we could do to help them." Don laughed a little.

The Emerald Ring

"Maybe we could find some kind of hidden treasure and then Mom and Dad wouldn't lose the farm." Steve asked, "What chance do we have of finding a hidden treasure stuck way out here." "I don't know", said Don, "but we can dream." "Sam told Bear, that's it." "What's it?" asked Bear? "A hidden treasure!" "What are you talking about?" "We could draw a treasure map and they could find it." "Ok. How do you know that they will try to find it?" "They're kids aren't they? It's bound to stir up their curiosity. Right now those kids are desperate and want to help their family. They'll try to find it." Sam said, "please Bear?" "Ok Sam. Let's go back to the cave and figure out how we are going to pull this off." "We can do it Bear." "If you say so. I can see right now Sam that our life is not going to be dull." "Of course not, whatever made you think it would be?" I really didn't think about it. Didn't you tell me to look at this as an adventure? Well, life is a big adventure and it is just what you make it."

Back at the cave Sam and Bear started looking around, trying to find something to make a treasure map out of. "We need to find something old so that they will think that it is real." "And where do you think that we are going to find that?" asked Bear. "We don't exactly have a store at our disposal." Sam walked over to where they found the home made stove. Sam was thinking that there might be something lying around that might work. Sam rummaged around and found an old canvas. "Perfect." She called to Bear. "What Sam?" "I found the perfect thing for the map." "Great, let's see. You're right, that will work." Bear looked around and found a pencil that had been left behind from whoever was there before. Sam and Bear sat down and planned the map. They drew a map starting a little ways past the farm house (so it would not look so conspicuous) to the cave. They put markers on the map so that they could identify where they were on the map. Each marker had a landmark all the way to the gold. Sam wrote a rhyme to go along with the map to help them along.

The rhyme went:

A cave was what you want to find,

Hidden well you must use your mind.

Follow the landmarks it made clear,

They will lead you very near.

The opening very hard to see, but like a mirrors reflection,

You can go right through, if you choose to enter.

The Emerald Ring

Into the waterfall you'll want to be,

To find a passageway you'll have to see.

A golden glow will lead you there,

Wait for the sunlight, a signal will guide you where.

Value is to the beholder, now guard it well,

To this land, you'll never have to sell.

This map will lead you to a treasure of old,

Follow it close and you'll find your gold.

"Sam this is really good." "Thanks Bear." "This just might work." "Sure it will Bear. You'll see. Ok now let's go find somewhere to plant it where they will find it. You know they have been over every inch of this place." I know."

"There's got to be a place. Let me think." Sam gazed around and tried to find a place where they could put the map. Bear and Sam slipped into the barn to look around. Bear noticed a loose piece of wood by the stairs and loosens it up a little more. They put the map into it and left just enough sticking out for the boys to find. Sam said, "I wonder how long it will take them to find it." "I'm hoping that they will find it tomorrow." "They will come in here and get the feed for the chickens in the morning. Let's cross our fingers." Let's head back to the cave. "

When they got back to the cave it was already starting to get dark. Bear built a fire so they could keep warm through the night. "Bear this has been a super day." Bear agreed. "We had better get some sleep in case those kids get an early start in the morning. Let's hope that they find the map."

The kids got up early the next morning and went out to the barn as usual to feed the live stock. Steve reached down to the loose board. He opened up the map and his heart started pumping. "Don come here quick." "What's the matter?" "Look, look what I found sticking out of that loose board. It's a treasure map." Don told Steve not to go getting all worked up. "You know It's probably not real." "How do you know? It could be real", said Steve. "Ok, ok let's have a look at it. It does look real", said Don. "Let's try to find it Don." "I don't know Steve." "Oh come on what can it hurt? It will be fun." "Ok after the chores are done and we eat we'll try to figure out the map." "Yeah!" yells Steve. "We're going to be rich." "Don't count your gold before you find it." Don told Steve, "If we do find it Mom and Dad won't lose the farm."

The Emerald Ring

After eating Steve and Don went out to the barn, got the map out and start trying to figure it out. "Ok Steve according to the map it starts here. Now all we have to do is follow the trail and look for the landmarks to make sure we are on the right track." "We'd better tell Mom that we're going to be playing jungle or something so she won't worry about us being gone for awhile." "Ok." They headed for the kitchen where Mom and Dad were. They told them that they are going to the river to play. "We will try to be back for lunch Mom." "Ok you boys be careful." "We will."

Out the door they went on their adventure. Little did they know that this adventure was going to change the rest of their lives forever. "Ok Steve let's see the map." Steve opened up the map and laid it on the stump.

"It looks like we need to go through those two posts of that broken down fence over there." They folded up the map and headed for the broken down fence. "Here we are. Now where do we go from here Don?" "Let's see the map again. It looks like we have to cross the corn field across from the old Oak tree." "Wow This is fun Don." They folded up the map again. "Aren't you excited Don?" "Of course I am." Steve and Don made their way to the corn

149

field. "Don I need to rest." "Ok Steve I'm pretty tired too." Don said, "This is a lot further than I thought." Don said, "I hope we find it before noon." "Me too!" said Steve. "Maybe we should have brought Dad with us." "We'll find it." "There's an apple tree ahead. We can pick an apple on the way." "Sounds good to me Steve!"

Steve and Don made their way to the apple tree. "There's the river Don." "I see it." "How much further is it?" "Not too far." "How are we going to get across the river?" "I don't know. We can figure that out when we get to it." Sam and Bear had already figured that out for them. They had made a raft and had laid it to the side so that they could find it. Steve and Don made it to the river and took another look at the map. "Ok Don, there's the Oak tree, the corn field, the apple tree, and across the river is the rock formation that was on the map. Let's look around, maybe we can figure out some way to get across the river. Maybe we can find a big log or something and float across it." Don saw the raft. It looked like it had been there for awhile. "Do you think it will float Don?" "I don't know. There is one way to find out." "Ok." Steve and Don pulled the raft onto the water. They waited a few minutes to see if the raft was going to float or not before they got on. "So far so good Steve." "Boy Don, this is like a

The Emerald Ring

real adventure. A raft, treasure map and clues,
there has just got to be gold." "Steve even if we
don't find any gold it sure was fun huh?" "It
sure was Don." "Ok Steve hop on. Let's get this
adventure on the way." Don and Steve headed
for the other side of the river. Lucky for them
this was the narrow part of the river going past
their farm.

   "We better pull the raft up so we don't lose
it." Over there was the rock formation. Three
rocks across from three more rocks with a
weeping willow in the middle. "Ok let's read the
rhyme again." *Follow the landmarks it's made
clear. They will lead you very near.* Don told
Steve that they had to be pretty close. "We're
exactly where the trail ends." The X was in the
weeping willow tree. The tree was against the
bluff.

   "I know Steve. What else does the rhyme
say?" *The opening hard to see but like a mirror
you can go straight through if you choose to
enter.* "I guess the only thing we can do is try
walking through the branches hanging down
from the tree." That is where the X is. "Maybe
the cave is in the bluff hidden behind the tree
branches", said Steve. "Maybe." They started
working their way through the branches. They
kept going and sure enough they found the

cave. Once inside the cave they started to look around. "Don I can't believe we haven't found this cave before. I thought we had been all over this place." "I know huh. Do you see anything?" "Looks like someone is camping out here. This looks fresh and here is a couple of back packs. We'd better not bother 'em." "Steve let's see what is in there." "Ok. Look a waterfall." "Cool. "

Wait a minute, "The rhyme had something about a waterfall in it. Where is the map?" They unfolded the map and repeated the rhyme again. *A cave is what you want to find. Hidden well you must use your mind. Into the waterfall you'll want to be, to find a passage way you'll have to see. A golden glow will lead you there. Wait for the sunlight, a signal will guide you where.* Steve says, "Ok sunlight. Do you see any sunlight Don?" "There is a sunbeam coming through that crack over there. Maybe the sunbeam is going to show us something. A golden glow will lead you there. Wait for the sunlight. What do you think Steve?" All of a sudden the sunbeam started getting brighter. They looked at each other. "Maybe." They start looking at the waterfall. "Look Don the waterfall is starting to glow and it is golden." "Yeah. Ok." "Ok." "Do you see anything Steve?" "No do you?" "No, keep looking." "There, over there by the wall of the cave." "I see it, I see it." "Hurry up let's get over there." They went over to the wall and start walking behind the waterfall. They called out to each other, "Steve." "Don." "Yeah.""What's back there?" "I don't know. I'm getting scared." "Me too Steve!" All the way in now they see the walls all sparkly and glowing with the golden glow like in the rhyme. "Is it gold Don?" "I don't know but it sure is pretty." "Yeah. We're rich, we're rich", yelled Steve. Don told Steve,We have got to be quiet. Remember we saw those back packs out there. We don't want anyone to hear us." Yeah, we found it." "Don says yeah."

Bear and Sam were hiding behind a large rock formation in the cave. They were watching them. Sam sneezed and the kids got scared and start to run. Bear jumped up and called them back. "Wait kids." "Wait we are your friends. We're not going to hurt you. We promise."Steve and Don turned around and headed back to where Sam and Bear were.

Sam and Bear explained to them how they found the gold while they were hiding out in the cave. They also told them they overheard them talking about how their parents were close to losing their farm. Bear told them how they came up with the idea of the map to get the boys to come there. "We wanted you to find the gold but we didn't want you to know about us. We didn't want to put you in any danger. We knew if you came up here and found the gold your parents wouldn't lose their farm." "Why are you hiding?" "It's a long story and we'll be happy to explain it to your parents. I'm afraid we have put you in danger by you discovering us too. "Woe, just like on TV." Bear told Steve not to get so excited. "Being Dead is not a good thing." "I know but nothing ever happens to us." "It did today. You found a gold mine." "Yeah! What do you want us to do now?"

"We need for you to go and get your parents and bring them here." "I don't think they will believe us." Take some gold with you and they will." How are we going to get gold off the wall?" "You're not." Bear told them to come over to the chest. "Look in there boys." They looked at each other and slowly lifted up the lid. They start screaming, "We're rich… we're rich! "Bear and Sam started laughing. "Do you think you can get them to come up here now?" "Sure." "We'll take a couple of nuggets with us and they will want to know where we found it." Remember one thing boys, you haven't seen us. Don't tell your Mom and Dad about us yet. We don't want to endanger them. "Thanks guys. We'll be back shortly." "Be careful." We

The Emerald Ring

will." "Bear why didn't you guys take the gold yourself?" "First it is not ours and second we don't need it." "Cool. You guys are alright!"

Back at the farmhouse Mom and Dad were getting a little worried. Mom told Dad, "They should have been back by now. Do you think something might have happened to them?" Dad assured her that they would be fine. "You know how those two boys are. Why I wouldn't be surprised if they didn't come in here any minute and tell us about some old pirates chest they found." "I know I just worry about them. Anything could happen to them." "I know", said Dad, "but I'm sure they are fine. If they aren't home soon I will go and look for them."

The back door slammed and in came the boys. Dad said, "See Mom what did I tell you." Mom said, "How many times do I have to tell you not to slam the door?" Ok, Mom, we won't do it anymore." "Of course not, at least until the next time." "Mom, Dad we've got something to tell you." "This sounds mysterious", Dad said. "You've got to come with us." "Where?" We found a gold mine right here on our property." Mom and Dad started laughing, "What did I tell you Mom?" "No, no we're serious." "You've got to come and see." "We're not going anywhere until we eat lunch." "You boys must have had quite an adventure today." "We sure did. We won't lose the farm now." "Now boys, I told you not to worry everything will be ok. Steve took out one of the nuggets; speechless for a moment, then they look at each other. "Son, where did you get this?" "We told you we found a gold mine."

"Maybe you boys had better start from the beginning." "Ok, it all started when we found the map." "What map?" "Steve found a map sticking out from a loose board in the barn. We decided to follow the map and see what we would find. We figured it wouldn't hurt. When we got to the hidden cave, we went in and read the map and found the gold. You got to see this Dad, it is totally awesome." Steve said, "We're rich." "Ok, ok boys, after we finish eating we will go and check it out." The boys were all excited and they could see a little hope in Dad's heart. They finished eating and headed for the cave. "Look at the map Dad. See, we followed all the landmarks and it led us here." "How did you get over to the other side?" "There's a raft here." "I see. Come on Mom get on." "I don't know about that. I'll stay here and you and Dad go." "No, you have to come too. You can do it Mom. We'll help you." They all get on the raft and floated to the other side.

The Emerald Ring

When they reached the other side Dad asked, "Boys where is the cave?" "Behind the tree." "Which tree?" "The weeping willow tree. You walk through the branches and into the cave. Well hidden huh?" It sure was. "Give me your hand Mom, I'll help you", said Steve. "I don't know. Are there any bats and snakes in there?" "I didn't see any."

"You're going to like It Mom." Mom said, "Ok, here we go." Don lead them into the cave. Mom said "This isn't so bad. It's not what I expected." "Pretty awesome huh Dad?" It sure is son. Now where is the gold?"

When the boys got back to the cave the sun had passed the hole and wasn't shinning towards the waterfall anymore. Steve said, "Don, where is the golden glow?" "What golden glow?" Dad asked. "The one in the rhyme. It gets you to the pathway behind the waterfall where the gold is."

Just then Bear called out to the boys. "We're here." "Who's that?" "It's ok Mom, Dad." "Follow our voice." Ok." "Come on Dad." They head toward their voices at the side of the cave by the waterfall. They could see Bear and Sam. Bear said "You must be Steve and Don's parents." "Yes we are." "We know you must have a lot of questions." "Yes, I don't know quite where to start." "We overheard your boys talking the other day about how you might lose your farm. When Sam and I stumbled onto the gold we were trying to figure out how to get you up here to discover the gold without knowing we were around." First things first." Bear told the parents to walk over to the chest. "Open it up." Steve and Don yelling, "Yeah Dad open the chest." Mom and Dad opened the chest. "Wow!" Bear told them that it was all theirs. "We don't understand." "This cave is on your property isn't it?" "Yes". "Then this all belongs to you." "Why didn't you guys take it and leave?" "We don't need it and it is not ours." Bear told them that he is a police detective. "We are hiding from some men that are chasing us. We finally got enough evidence to put them away. They found out that we have the evidence and started" trying to catch us and silence us if you know what I mean. When the bridge washed out we started walking and ended up in this cave. Lucky for us. "

"After we had rested a little we started checking out the area around us when we discovered the gold. I had gone down to the river to catch some fish when I saw your two boys. Sam and I slipped down to the house to check you out when we heard your boys talking about you losing your farm. So we made the map and the boys came and found the gold and here you are." "I see." "Don't feel bad. This should help. Does your deed have mineral rights or ore rights included in it?" "I don't know I never paid any mind to it. If it does all this gold is yours and no one not even the government or anyone else can take it away from you. Do you know where your deed is?" "Yes." The kid's parents invited Sam and Bear to go back to the house with them.

"Well I don't know Mam." "Don't call me Mam. My name is Brenda and my husband's name is Carter." "Now you two get your selves together and let's go." "I'll fix you something to eat." "Sounds good to me Bear." "Carter I'll check your deed and see if you have any mineral and ore rights on it if you want." "Great!" They put some of the gold into the back packs and headed back to the house.

Back at the house Brenda fixed them something to eat. Carter found the deed and showed it to Bear. "Carter as best as I can make out, you have all the rights above and below ground. The gold is as good as yours. I'll call a friend of mine and tell him that you are on your way to register it." "Thanks Bear. I don't know how to thank you." "Just save your farm." "I will. This land had been in the family for generations. How could it be taken away from you then?" "I don't know but for the last two years there has been one thing after another. First they tried to say there were back taxes. I proved them wrong on that. Now they are trying to say that there wasn't a will and that it belongs to the government. I found the will the other day and Dad even had it notarized." "Great!"

"I knew something have must be going on. I bet they know about the gold somehow and they are trying to run me off before I find it." "You could be right. We never had any troubles before." "After you file there is nothing that they can do. Actually there is nothing they can do now. It's on your property." "Be careful. I'm going to leave you my phone number in case you have any more problems." "Hopefully they will let up now especially when they find out that you are my friend. "

Chapter 11: Meeting the Family

"I'm going to call my Uncle and have him get in touch with Larry, a friend of mine. He will fly down and pick us up and take us to the ranch." Your friend has an airplane?" "No, I do." "Sam asked, "You do?" "Yes. I enjoy flying when I can find the time and it sure comes in handy at the ranch. It is a lot of territory to cover if you're looking for something." "Your Uncle fly's too?" "Yes, but I don't want him coming after us in case there is any trouble. Larry will come and get us. He loves to fly. He will be here before you know it." Bear made the call. He told Bear that he would be there in a couple of hours. "Great!"

After talking with Brenda and Carter for awhile they were sorry to have to leave them. Bear reminds them in case someone comes looking for them that they haven't seen us. "Just pretend that you don't have a clue what they are talking about. These men are dangerous." Steve told Bear, "You can count on us. If you guys ever get a chance, come and see us at the ranch." Brenda says, "We will." "Look there's a plane." "Yep, that's mine alright." "Wow that's quite a plane." "Thanks. It does its job." His buddy landed the plane and jumped out to see him. "How you doing ole buddy? I haven't seen you for quite awhile." They shook each others hand and gave each other a hug. "What is going on? It must be pretty important to have me fly up here to get you." "I guess you could say that. I've got two men hot on my trail trying to stop me from turning in states evidence on them." I see. Pretty heavy. Well then, let's load you up and get you out of here." "Wait a minute Larry. I want to introduce you to some fine people. Larry, This is Carter and his wife Brenda." "It's nice to meet you." Then Larry noticed Sam. "Ok Bear, who is this lovely creature?" "This is the woman I'm going to marry." "Hot dog." "I can't believe it. Someone has finally landed you. Now can we finally get out of here so we can make sure you two make it to the altar?" They all laughed while getting into the plane. Larry yelled out, "Carter, Brenda nice to have met you. Catch you again sometime." Bear told Carter that they would fly over the farm to see if anyone was snooping around and if it was ok they would tip the wing as they flew back over. "Bye." They all waved goodbye.

"Sam you're going to like the ranch. He's told me a little about it. It sounds really nice." "There aren't many that can hold a candle to Bear's Ranch. It's the best."

The Emerald Ring

Bear fell asleep right after take off. Meanwhile Sam asked Larry "How long have you known Bear"? "A long time! We go way back. There wasn't anything that I wouldn't do for the Bear." After flying for some time they made it to Bears Ranch. "Sam, take a look out there." "What is it?" "Did you see where that fence entrance was?" "Yes." "Well that is where Bears Ranch starts." "Oh ok." "He said he had some horses but he didn't know how many." It's hard telling now." "That's what he said. How come? "I'll show you." Larry pulled the plane to the right and flew over to where some of Bears horses were. "Look down there... Hundreds and hundreds of horses. He lost count a long time ago. Last count he had it was about 1,500. Do you like horses Sam?" "Oh yes. I thought I had a lot of horses until I saw these." "Sam that's not all of them. It isn't?" "No, there are horses all over this ranch." Bear woke up. Bear told Larry that Sam owns a fine horse ranch. "Well here we are." Larry landed the plane and they got out. Larry taxied the plane to the hanger and refueled it.

"Well Sam, here we are, what do you think?" "Bear it's just to amazing for words. I never imagined anything like this." "Let's go in and I'll take you to your room and you can clean up and get a little rest." "Ok Bear, that sounds pretty good right now." "I'll come and get you when it is time for supper." "Thanks Bear." Bear gets Sam all settled in and then left to find his uncle. He headed out to the barn. "I figured that I'd find you out here. Where is Aunt Rosemary?" "She went into town to get a few things." "I have a surprise for you." You do? What is it?" "You're going to have to wait until supper." "So what brings you back here?" I've got to keep a low profile for awhile. I have to turn states evidence in on some guys and they are not too happy about it. It is going to put them away for a long time. They found out that I have the evidence on them and they are looking for me." "I see." "As soon as Bobbie has everything ready for trial she'll call me and I can testify against them. Uncle Walter, I'm going to clean up and lay down for awhile." "You go ahead Bear. Sounds like you have had a rough couple of days." "Sure have, tell Aunt Rosemary that I'll be down for supper with the surprise I have for you guys." "OK. "

Bear left a message in the kitchen for Aunt Rosemary that she would be having two more for supper. Bear went up to his room. On his way to his room he peeked in on Sam and saw her sleeping. He was thinking to himself, *I'm the luckiest man in the world.*

The Emerald Ring

Bear went into his room. He got himself cleaned up and sat on his bed for a minute thinking and remembering his Grandmother. He had a special relationship with her. He had forgotten about the special agreement they had made before she died. Thinking of her had brought it back to him what she had told him to do when the time came. *Well Grandmother, I guess this is the right time.* He walked over to the top of his dresser and in the top drawer he pulled out a ring box. He opened it up and inside it was a beautiful Emerald Ring. The ring had a one carat emerald in the middle and two carats' of diamonds around it. *She told me that this ring was a very special ring. When the right time comes the secret of this ring will be revealed to you. Give it to the woman you love. It has special powers and will protect you. Your love for each other will increase its power. I don't know about all that power stuff but it is a beautiful ring and I haven't had time to get her an engagement ring so I guess this will do.*

Bear rested for awhile then went in to check on Sam. She was lying across the bed resting but awake. "Hi Sam, you ok? How you holding up?" "I guess ok." "I told Uncle Walter and Aunt Rosemary that I had a surprise for them at supper time. I am going to tell them that we're getting married. They will be so surprised." "Do you think they will like me?" "Of course they will. This is going to make them so happy. You have no idea. Sam I have something for you." "What is it?" "I hope you like it, it belonged to my Grandmother. She told me that when I fell in love that I was supposed to give this ring to her." Sam opened the box and saw the beautiful Emerald Ring. Sam gasped for a minute. Bear asked her, "Are you alright?" "Yes it is just so beautiful!" "Here, let me help you put it on." "Ok. It looks like it was made just for you. A perfect fit." Bear held her in his arms and they kissed. While they were embracing each other a ghostly image appeared in the mirror of the dresser in the room. They heard a voice and looked up. Sam held Bear a little tighter. Bear told Sam, "It's my Grandmother." She gave them a message. *"Be true to yourselves and to each other. Love is the most powerful force on Earth. Nothing can touch it. I'm very pleased. You now possess the key, a powerful force which true love unlocks."* All of a sudden she left as quickly as she came. Bear told Sam that he didn't understand but he knew that someday it would all come clear. "I know she came for a reason and to let me know she approves of my lady. She will always be with us."

Rosemary got Bears note about two more

The Emerald Ring

for dinner. Rosemary asked Walter if he knew where Larry was? "He left and said he had some things he had to take care of." "Why?" "Bear left me a note that there would be two more for supper and I thought it was Larry. I wonder what he has up his sleeve?" "He said he has a surprise for us at supper." "I wonder what it is? I haven't a clue."

Well supper was almost ready so I guess we'll find out soon. I guess. He said he was going to lay down for awhile. I'm going to go and get cleaned up for supper. Ok Walter.

Back in Sam's room Bear took her out onto the balcony. "You can see for miles from here. Sam as far as you can see is ours." "That's a lot of land." "Yes it is." "Do you think Baby would be happy here?" "Well I reckon, Bear told Sam "I guess that is one thing we're going to have to talk about. Where do we want to live, my ranch or yours?" "I always thought I would live on my ranch. I never gave it any thought. If we lived here who would take care of my ranch?" "You've got Jake and from what I can tell Shamrock and Mamie are getting pretty chummy." "I know huh." "Well we'll see. Are you ready to go down stairs?" "I guess."

Bear and Sam headed down the beautiful wide curved stairwell. "After we eat and I introduce you to everyone I'll show you around." They headed for the dining room. Uncle Walter headed down at the same time. "Well Bear who is this? Where have you been hiding her?" "I'll tell you in a minute, where is Aunt Rosemary?" She'll be here in a minute." In walked Aunt Rosemary. "Well Bear, where's our surprise?" Just as the words were coming out of her mouth she saw Sam. "Aunt Rosemary, Uncle Walter I'd like to introduce you to the lady I'm going to marry." "Oh praise God. Come here let me look at you." They gave her a big hug and welcome her to the family. "You don't know how long we have been praying for this. We are so happy for you both. When are you getting married?" "We don't know yet. There is so much to do and decide." "He just asked me a couple of days ago." "I see. Are you going to get married here?" "We don't know." "Calm down Aunt Rosemary." "I will, I just want you to hurry up and get married. I don't want anything to happen to change it." "There is nothing in the world that would keep us from getting married." Aunt Rosemary started crying. I'm so happy. Uncle Walter said, "let's eat!" Bear chimes in, "I agree." They all sat down to eat. Rosemary asked Sam, "How did you ever get him to ask you to marry him?" "I don't know." Bear chimed in, "Actually Aunt

The Emerald Ring

Rosemary she didn't and I want to marry her before she changes her mind." Bear said, "Timing has a lot to do with it." Sam said, "I guess you might say he swept me off my feet. I had to hurry up because there is another fella after her too." "I'll bet there is says Uncle Walter. You're lucky to catch such a fine looking filly." "I know, but praise God I have and I want to spend the rest of my life with her. I think it is time for me to retire and settle down." Aunt Rosemary started to cry again.

"Are you going to come back here to live?" "That's something that we're going to have to talk about. Sam has a nice horse ranch and I know she doesn't want to give it up. It means a lot to her. We have a lot of things to work out." "I was just wondering. We sure would love having you around here." "If you guys will excuse us I'm going to show Sam around the ranch. Are you ready Sam?" "Sure Bear."

They were headed for the stables when one of the men working for them stopped them. "I've got everything taken care of Bear. It should arrive here sometime this evening." "Thanks a lot! I owe you one." "You don't owe me anything. I'd do anything for you Bear, you know that." "I know but I want you to know I really appreciate it." Ok." *Sam is going to be so surprised. I can't wait.* Sam asked, "What was all that?" "Oh nothing, I just had him taking care of something for me. He wanted to let me know it was all taken care of." "That's good. You know there must be a lot more to you than meets the eye." "What do you mean?" "Every person we come in contact with seems to love you to pieces and would do anything for you." "It's really nothing. I just helped them along here and there." I can't wait to hear their story."

"Bear these horses are magnificent. Thank you." "That means a lot coming from you. Would you like to ride around the ranch or fly?" "I don't know. If we ride there is no way that we could see it all." "You're right there." "Ok, you talked me into it, let's fly." "Good, I don't get to fly much and I have been dying to get some flying in." "Bear why ever do you stay away from all this?" "I didn't have anyone to share it with so I did the second thing I love next, being a detective. I'm glad I did, I found you. "

"Being a police detective doesn't even come close to all this." "It does if you don't have anyone to share it with. Maybe now ...we'll give it some thought." Sam told Bear, "Lets ride now." They headed back to the house. Then they headed for the stable after landing. "Which one do you want to ride?" "The buckskin is mine and his name is Cherokee." "How about that one?" "Ok, I'll saddle her up for you." "She sort of reminds me of Star a little." "Pick you out a saddle." "This one is fine." "Ok just give me a minute." Bear got the horses all saddled up and they started to mount up when Aunt Rosemary intercomed Bear. "What is it Aunt Rosemary?" "There is a long distant call for you." "Ok I'll take it out here. Sam if you want to get a feel for her, ride her around outside and I'll meet you out there in a minute." "Ok Bear." Bear took the phone call. "It's Jim the Veterinarian. I've got everything ready on this end Bear, but I wasn't going to ship Baby anywhere until I heard from you. If anything happened to Baby." I know. It will be ok " "Bear, Sam will be so surprised." Bear told Jim that he and Sam are going to get married. "Congratulations. It's about time that Sam settles down. I'm glad it is to you Bear." "Thanks Jim. Talk to you later."

Bear met Sam outside and they rode for awhile taking in all the land, horses and cattle that Bear had. They were almost back to the house when they stopped for a minute. Looking down at the house Bear asked Sam if she had thought any more about where she would like to live? "Living here would be great but I sure would miss the ranch." "I know." "We can bring Baby and Star here if you want. You know Jake can take care of the ranch for you and Shamrock is taking care of Mamie. You don't have to make up your mind yet. We have plenty of time." "Bear, it sounds like maybe you have already made up your mind." "No comment. We're going to live wherever you want. I want you to be happy. I can be happy in either place. "

"Look Bear there is a plane coming in. Who's flying your plane?" "Larry. He is doing me a favor. Actually I have him bringing you a surprise." "A surprise for me?" "Yep." Sam said, "Let's hurry up and get down there. The plane is landing." Sam and Bear tied up the horses and got ready to meet the plane. "Bear what in the world could you have gotten me for a surprise that would require a plane." "You'll see." The plane door opened and Jim walked out." "Well hi Him. You flew Jim out here?" "Yeah, but that's not the surprise."

Jim went back into the plane and brought out Baby. Baby walked out a little groggy until she saw Sam. All of a sudden Baby started on a dead run straight for Sam. "Look out", said Larry. "Trust me", said Bear. Baby jumped on her and started licking her. "Well I'll be", said Larry. "Bear ,when did you have time to do all

172

The Emerald Ring

this." Sam walked over to him and told Bear, "I sure do love you." Then all of a sudden Baby jumped up on Bear. "It's a good thing Baby likes you Bear or you might be in trouble." "I know. Jim would you like to stay a couple of days with us." "Thanks, I sure would but I really need to get back." "Ok." "See you guys later. Oh by the way Sam, congratulations." Larry shut the door and taxied to the runway.

Sam was so excited to see Baby. Bear and Sam played with her for awhile and then headed for the house. Uncle Walter came out and said, "What do we have here?" "Uncle Walter, This is Baby.

This is Sam's pet cougar." "Well it's nice to meet you Baby." Baby just looked at him. "Wait till' your Aunt Rosemary sees you. Aunt Rosemary loves animals. She'd take in all the critters if it were possible." "Sounds like Rosemary and I have a lot in common." "You two will get along alright." "Bear and I won't stand a chance around here with you two women", said Uncle Walter. Bear and Uncle Walter started laughing.

Sam and Bear took Baby into the house. "It's time to meet Aunt Rosemary. Bear calls out, "Aunt Rosemary." "I'm in the kitchen." They headed for the kitchen. Bear told Aunt

Rosemary to close her eyes for a minute. "Ok Bear." "Ok now you can open them." "Oh my goodness child. Where ever did you get such a fine looking animal?" "I've had her since she was a baby. Something had killed her mother so I brought it home and took care of it the best I could. We kind of bonded. She thinks I'm her mother." "She is beautiful Sam." Baby took to Aunt Rosemary right away. "What is her name?" "Baby." Bear told Aunt Rosemary about the special room she had fixed up for her next to her bedroom. "Wow, that sounds like quite a room." "You haven't heard anything yet."

In came Walter and they all sat down and talked for awhile. Uncle Walter suggested that they have a cook out so that everyone could meet Sam. In came Dusty, Rosemary and Walter's son. "What's up guys?" "Dusty", said Uncle Walter, "I want you to meet Sam. Bear and Sam are getting married." "Welcome to the family Sam."

"The cook out is a good idea", said Aunt Rosemary. Aunt Rosemary was always ready to cook and didn't need an excuse to have people over. She enjoyed feeding people and having fellowship with them. "I'll start getting it ready first thing in the morning." "I'll get started on getting the meat ready for the get together",

The Emerald Ring

said Walter. "How many people do you think will be here?" "Oh on such short notice I guess we can't expect too many." Uncle Walter said, "I think we can count on at least 50 or 60." "Oh my goodness", said Sam. "That's quite a get together." "Not really usually we have two or three hundred." "I see", said Sam. Aunt Rosemary says she had better go and get some rest because she had a lot to do tomorrow. Sam offered to help her but Aunt Rosemary told her that she was the guest of honor and that she should just enjoy the get together. Dusty says, "Dad I'll help you get the fire wood together." "That would be great Dusty." "Tomorrow you are going to meet a lot of friends and neighbors." "Ok I guess I had better turn in too." Bear walked her to her room. "I like your Uncle Walter and Aunt Rosemary." "They like you too." "How do you know?" "Are you kidding? If they didn't they wouldn't be planning to show you off." "I don't know. It'll be ok, trust me." "Ok Bear. What am I going to wear? We really didn't have a chance to pack when we left." "We'll take care of that tomorrow." Bear gave her a big hug and kiss and told her that he would see her in the morning. "I'm surprised you're not staying in my room tonight." "Believe me it was heavy on my mind but it wouldn't be right. We're not married yet and I'm not going to be disrespecting you around my family." "You are so thoughtful Bear. Definitely a one of a kind." "You're very special to me Sam." "I know. And you're very special to me too." "You've got Baby to keep you company." "I sure do. Bear you're just a sweetheart." "Good night Sam." "Good night Bear, I love you." "I love you too stuff."

Bear went to his room, laid across the bed and tried to figure things out. There were a lot of things to work out before they could get married. They had to go to court and testify so those men could get locked up. They had to decide where they were going to live and make arrangements on what to do if they decided to live there. *I sure do wish we were walking down the aisle tomorrow.*

Back in Sam's room she was trying to decide on where she wanted to live. I wonder if Jake would still want to run the ranch for me if I decided to live here. I'm sure he would. I could bring Star here when we go back to testify in court. I sure do like it here. Who knows, maybe Shamrock and Mamie will hit it off and with Jake they could run the ranch for me. That would work. She drifts off to sleep. Tomorrow was going to be a big day for Sam. Bear peaks in and sees Sam laying there with Baby snuggled up to her.

Early the next morning, Uncle Walter and Aunt Rosemary were busy getting ready for the get together. Sam and Bear got up and had some breakfast. Sam asked Rosemary, "Are you sure that I can't help you?" "No Hun, I have everything under control." "I don't see how you do it." "I've been doing this for so many years that it all just comes together. Today you're going to meet a lot of people. I just want you to have a good time. Bear said, "That's my job and I'll make sure she has a good time. I'm not going to let her out of my sight."

Bear asked Sam what she would like to do today. "I don't care." "We can take it easy by the pool or go riding or if you want we can take a walk." Sam interrupts, "Bear should we give Bobbie a call to see what is going on?" "I had planned on doing that this morning. We can do it now if you like." "Ok." Bear called Bobbie to see if there had been any progress in getting a court date. Bobbie let them know that the Judge had set a court date for the trial in two days. "The Judge did something very unusual. He had the inquiry last night at 10:00 and set the court date. He wants to get this taken care of and not be drawn out. We could have this all behind us by the end of the week." "That sounds good to me. I was going to try to get a hold of you this afternoon. Bobbie we are in Oklahoma now." "Good. I'll buy tickets for you guys the morning of the trial." "That won't be necessary. I can fly us back myself." "Whatever you want to do", said Bobbie. "Just let me know when you'll be here and I will send a car for you." "Ok. I'll talk to you later." "Sam you want to talk to Bobbie?" "That's ok. Just tell her the good news." "Oh Bobbie, guess what." "Sam and I are getting married." "Wow! That's great!" "Tell her I'll talk to her later. Ok?"

"Sam, Day after tomorrow we have to fly back and testify. It'll all be over with soon. Then we can get married." "I can't wait." "You are going to have to. There is so much to do. It takes time to plan a wedding." "I know. Aunt Rosemary and Mamie will help you." "I know. How about two weeks from tomorrow we get married? If something happens we can pick another date." "Ok Bear. Now how about that walk?"

Sam and Bear walked around the grounds for awhile. Sam noticed all the hustle and bustle of everyone getting ready for the get together that evening. Bear looked at Sam. "This is all for you." They headed back into the

The Emerald Ring

kitchen when Sam noticed all the meat. "Uncle Walter that's enough meat to feed an Army", said Sam. "Not really there won't be any left when everyone is gone."

"I guess we'd better go and get ready, people will be coming soon." Sam asked, "What do people wear to these get together's?" "Dress like you were going out with your friends on Friday night." "Great, this is my kind of get together. Do you think they will like me Bear?" "Are you kidding? You are a very special lady and I am a lucky man to have you. Everyone is going to love you. Believe me I'm going to be keeping my eye on you." "Oh Bear." "Get ready and we'll go downstairs." "Bear I don't have any clothes remember. I'm sorry Sam, I wasn't thinking. I'll take care of that in a minute. Write down your sizes and I'll be back in a minute." Bear took the paper to Aunt Rosemary. Aunt Rosemary's daughter was the same size as Sam so she brought some of her clothes in for her. "Sam, I wish you would have said something sooner." "I'm sorry I don't want to be a bother." "You're no bother. Do you like any of these?" "These are really nice Aunt Rosemary." "If you would like to see something else my daughter's room is the third door down the hall on the right. Go in there and use anything you want. She is not here much."

"Thanks Rosemary." "You're welcome. Now get dressed and let's get this show on the road." "Thanks Bear. I should be ready in about an hour." "See you then Stuff. Take your time."

Sam got ready and Bear came to escort her down the stairs. I'"m ready Bear." "You're beautiful Sam." "You're not so bad yourself. Do I have to keep my eye on you Bear? How many of these women are going to try to take you away from me?" "There might be a few that might try to ruffle your feathers but don't pay any attention to them. I won't. I am the one you asked to marry you." "Good girl."

Guests had already started arriving. Bear had started introducing her to the ones that had already started arriving. "Well Sam, are you having fun?" "Yes but I'm not used to being the center of attention." "Sam you are always the center of attention where ever you are. You just do not realize it." "Oh Bear." "It's true Sam. When I saw you at the Silver bullet every man in the place had his eye on you. People just love you Sam." "I hope so. I do like people and I like helping them even more." "That's what makes you so special. You are genuine."

About that time the music started. "Bear asked Sam, "Would you like to dance?" "I can't believe it, we even have music too?" "It's not a

real get together without music." Everyone
started to dance. After the first dance the men
kept cutting in on Bear. He expected that
though. Sam would always be returned back
to Bear and reminded that he was a lucky man.
Uncle Walter got everyone's attention for the
big announcement. "Friends, friends I have an
announcement to make!" "There's someone I
want to introduce you to. I know that some of
you have already met her. Bear, Sam, come up
here." Sam and Bear made their way up to the
front. "This is Sam, she and Bear are going to
get married very soon. I'd like you all to
welcome her to our family." Everyone cheered
and clapped their hands. Sam thanked them
and told them that she would probably be
seeing them very soon. Bear took over and told
their guests that they were getting married in
two weeks. The guests got even more excited.
Uncle Walter and Aunt Rosemary came over
and congratulated them. "Sam I sure hope you
let me help you with your wedding plans. I
know you probably have people who want to
but I really would like to help." "Of course you
can help Rosemary. I'd like you and Mamie to
get together and the three of us can probably
pull this off. Seems like Bear is in a hurry and
not giving me much time." Sam noticed Dusty
having a good time. "Look Bear all those girls

around Dusty. I'll bet he loves that." Bear said, "He's quite the charmer alright."

Finally Sam and Bear bid everyone good night and headed back to the house. "Bear I just love your family and friends. They are really nice people." "I can tell they really like you too." "I'm glad. I've been thinking Bear that if we could get Star out here and find a way to keep my ranch; I'd love to live out here." "That's great Sam. Are you sure?" "You're not saying that because of me are you?" "No I really mean it. "

"What about your job?" "I don't need that job anymore. I have you. I plan on spending the rest of my life making you happy. I don't need anything else." Bear told Sam, "After the trial we'll start working on getting things worked out, Ok?" "Ok."

Bear kissed her good night and headed for his room. Sam got ready for bed. Sam said, "Hi Baby girl. I sure do love you." Baby snuggled up to her. All of a sudden a strange feeling came over Sam. Something was going to happen. Bear sensed her feelings and came into the room. "Sam are you ok?" "I don't know." "What's wrong?" "I can't put my finger on it but something bad is going to happen. I don't think I should go to the court house." "We

The Emerald Ring

have to testify." "I know." "Is there some other way I could testify and not be there?" "I guess but I'm not going to let anything happen to you. It will be ok. Trust me." "I've learned to trust my instincts and something is going to happen to me." "It'll be ok Sam. It's probably everything that is happening to you right now." "You think so?" "Of course." "Ok. Good night Bear." "Good night Sam." "Bear would you lay across the bed until I fall asleep." "Of course I will." Bear laid there with Sam and Baby. Sam just couldn't shake the feeling that something was going to happen to her. All the next day and that night she couldn't help but worry. Sam told Bear again that she was worried. "I will be with you the whole time." "I know. You don't understand Bear. I can't explain it but I just know when something bad is going to happen. I had this feeling when my Grandfather died." "I'll call ahead and have them increase the security. Ok."

The next morning Sam and Bear got ready to board the plane. Aunt Rosemary and Uncle Walter were right there to see them off. "Now you hurry up and get back here Sam. We've got a wedding to plan." "We will. I want to thank you all for everything." We enjoyed having you. Good luck guys." Dusty came running. "Bear, here comes Dusty", said Sam. Dusty gave them each a big hug. Dusty told Sam, "I'm sure glad you're going to be a part of the family. Now you hurry and get back here ok?" They all laughed as Sam and Bear got into the plane. They took off and were on their way. Bear radioed the airport and told them to contact Bobbie for him and to gives her their E.T.A. He explained their situation to them. "Will do partner. Bear knew the guys at the airport so they were happy to do that for him."

As soon as they landed sure enough Bobbie had a car waiting for them. Uncle Don was in the car to meet them. "Hey. I hear congratulations are in order." Uncle Don gave Sam a big hug. "Thanks Uncle Don. You don't look so happy Sam. This isn't like you. What's the matter?" I don't know. I just have this feeling that something bad is going to happen to me." "Tell me about it on the way to the court house." They got in and headed for the court house. Uncle Don peaked at his watch. "Looks like we are going to make it just in time. Now Sam, tell me about this feeling you have." "Remember when Grandfather died. I got that same feeling then. I really can't explain it." "Sam, Bear and I are going to be with you through the whole trial and you know how protective we are of you. They have all the people involved with Janex in custody so there is nothing to worry about." "Ok Uncle Don. I hope you are right."

They pulled up to the court house and they saw several police officers waiting there to escort them into the court room. Uncle Don said, "See Sam, this won't take long. We will go in and testify and then come right out. It will be over with before you know it. Then you can concentrate on the wedding." "Sounds good to me." They pulled up to the curb and the police helped them out of the car. Sam looked at Bear and said, "Bear I love you." She gave Uncle Don a hug. On their way up the steps they heard a gun shot. Quickly Bear looked up. Sam turned around and looked at Bear with tears in her eyes and fell down to the steps. "Somebody call an ambulance quick. Sam, Sam, Bear lifts her up into his arms. I'm sorry Sam. Why didn't I listen to you?" "Bear you go on in and testify and I'll get Sam to the hospital. You know that is what Sam would want you to do. You can meet us at the hospital. We will probably get there the same time." Ok but hurry and get her to the hospital. I'll be there as fast as I can." Quickly the police apprehended the shooter and took him into custody while Sam was on her way to the hospital.

Bear testified and headed for the hospital.

By the time he got there Mamie and Shamrock were there too. Uncle Don filled Bear in on what they were doing. "Sam is in surgery and they are doing everything that can be done Bear. All we can do right now is wait and pray." "It seems like they are taking forever. What are they doing in there?, asked Bear. "Everything they can." A couple of hours later Sterling showed up and Mamie met him. "How is she doing Mamie?" "We don't know yet."

"Everything that can be done is being done." "I came by to tell Sam that the men she was after are being put away for a long time. After it was over I heard what had happened to Sam and I had to come." I know Sterling." "You see that guy over there. Yes. his name is Bear."" It is a long story but Sam agreed to marry him before she got shot." "I see." "Sam wasn't really interested in having anyone in her life right now and in the last month you two popped up and started courting her. You guys messed up her world. I know she cares a lot about you Sterling."

"At the trial I saw him testify. He was the head of the investigation." "Yes, he and Sam were working on it together." "Oh. Sam told me she didn't have anyone in her life right now." "She didn't think she did and along came Bear.

The Emerald Ring

She didn't know what to do. He saved her from your burning building. Her hero huh?" "I do know though that you mean an awful lot to her." "I see."

Bear walked over to Mamie. "Bear I'd like to introduce you to Sterling." "Excuse us a minute we'll be right back." They walked over to the side a little and Mamie told Bear to cool it." "What do you mean?" "You know Sterling loves Sam just as much as you do and is hurting too. Sam had agreed to marry you so do you think you could be friends at least until she gets out of the hospital? I think Sam would like that." "Ok Mamie, you're right. We have got to think of Sam right now."

Mamie and Bear walked back over to where Sterling was and Bear asked Sterling if he would like to stay awhile. "I'd like that Bear." "Thank you." Just then the doctor came out and told them the room number that they had moved Sam to. It was in intensive care. Bear asked, "Can I see her?" "Not right now. Sam has a long way to go. We got the bullet out but she had gone into a coma. All we can do now is wait. It is all up to her now." Bear started crying. Sterling put his arms around Bear and tried to console him. "She'll be ok Bear. She has a lot to live for. You two are going to be married and have lots of kids." Bear looked up at Sterling and said, "I'm ok. Thanks Sterling." Mamie walked over to them and winked at Bear and he smiles at Mamie. They all went into the waiting room together.

Sterling asked if there was anything that he could do. But there wasn't. Bear made his way into the Chapel to pray and ask God to please let Sam live. He meditated there for hours and told Sterling that he had to leave for a little while, but that he would be back. "You know under the circumstances I really shouldn't like you but you've been a real friend. I'll see you in a little bit. "

Sterling left and Bear went out to Mamie to see if she had heard anything yet. "Not really Bear. The longer she is in the coma the less chance she has of making it back. I'm getting worried Bear." Bear went to find one of the doctors to ask if there might be something that they might be missing. "I know it is hard Bear, but all we can do is wait." Bear was just beside himself. In walked Aunt Rosemary, Uncle Walter and Uncle Don. Uncle Don had gone to get them from the airport. They called to Bear. Bear hurried over to them and filled them in on what had happened. They tried to assure Bear that everything was going to be alright. Mamie walked over to them and Bear introduced them to her. "You are the one who called us." "Yes, I hope you don't mind Bear. I thought you should have some family with you right now." "That's fine Mamie." "I wasn't thinking. All I can think about is Sam." "I know." In walked Sterling. Bear walked over to him and told him that there hadn't been any changes. "Sterling I need for you to do something for me." "Anything Bear. There might be something that I can do? What? I'll do anything to help you help Sam Bear." "I can't tell you right now but I need you to come with me right now." "Where to?" They walked to the Chapel. "I need you to stay in here and pray like you have never prayed before. Don't leave until you hear from me. Promise me." "I promise." "I'll be back soon and if it works Sam will be back with us." "What are you going to do?" "I can't tell you yet, just do as I have asked, please." "I will Bear." "Remember don't leave here Sam needs us both right now."

Bear went out to the waiting area and told everyone that he would be back shortly and that Sterling was in the Chapel. He asked them to keep praying while he was gone. After they promised him he left. He wouldn't tell them where he was going. Bear got into his car and headed for the reservation. When he got there he found the Chief.

Bear told the Chief everything that had happened and asked if there was anything that he could do. "White man has done everything that he can do. Chief, she is still in a coma. Please help me."

The Chief sat quietly for awhile and then told Bear that he would have to go on a long journey. He must look for her spirit. Her spirit wasn't going to be easy to find. The spirit realm is different and he only had a short time to find her.

"If you don't find her before your journey ends you have to come back or you could be lost to the other side. You will be dead to this side. If you do find her spirit you have to convince her to return to her body. You have to try before your journey ends." "Are you ready to take this journey?" "I am."

The Chief began by throwing something into the fire. A big puff of white smoke rose up to the top of the teepee. Bear was sitting on one side of the fire and the chief was on the other. The Chief threw something else into the fire and blew something at Bear. Bear entered into his journey.

Bear kept calling for Sam's spirit trying to

The Emerald Ring

reach her. He heard nothing. He kept calling, "Sam, Sam please answer me. I love you. Where are you? I need you please come back. Sam please help me find you. Where are you? Please Sam." Bear starts to see images of Sterling praying for her. "Sam you have got to come back. There are so many people who need you and love you." Bear hears a faint cry. "Bear." He could barely hear her. "Keep calling me. Sam I can barely hear you. Sam, Sam." Then Bear heard her voice a little louder. "Sam I can hear you a little better. Keep calling for me." Soon he could see her. Bear reached out for her but couldn't quite reach her yet. "Sam please reach for my hand. Please take it. I don't have much time." Just as she was about to be drawn away, she took Bears hand. He lead her back to her body in the hospital room and tried to get back. Unfortunately his time had run out, but he could still hear the chief chanting. He followed the chant and made it back. He looked at the Chief and told him that he had found her. "You must go to her now."

Just as Bear was ready to depart a strange man appeared out of nowhere. The Chief thinking that this man must be part of his journey didn't say anything. Bear thinking that the Chief knew who he was didn't say anything. The Chief and Bear shrugged their shoulders at each other as being confused and then the man asked Bear to take his hand. Bear looked at the Chief and the Chief told him to go ahead. Bear took his hand and was immediately transported into Sam's room. Once there the man disappeared. Bear confused but happy to be in Sam's room forgot about the man for a minute. Bear called, "Sam, Sam, Sam. Can you hear me?" Sam opened her eyes and looked at Bear. "Oh Sam, he reached down to hold her and then called the doctor in. "Doc, Doc, come in here quick." The Doctor examined her and told Bear that she was going to be fine. "Oh praise God."

While the Doctor was letting everyone in to see her Bear went into the Chapel to see Sterling. "We did it. Sam is going to be alright. Let's go and see Sam." They headed into the hospital room. Bear stopped and motioned Sterling to go on in. "Hi Sam." "Hi Sterling." "I heard about you and Bear." You're getting a terrific guy." "Yeah. I think so too." "I hope we will still be able to be friends." Bear walked in and Sam was a little nervous. She saw Bear shake Sterling's hand and give him a hug. Bear thanked Sterling again. "Sterling I have another favor to ask you." "Sure what is it? "I'd like you to be my best man." "I'd be honored Bear." By this time Sam was totally confused. Sterling reached down and gave Sam a kiss on the forehead and told her to take it easy. "Sam we can still be friends. I'll check in on you later." "Ok Sterling."

"Alone at last. Sam you scared me. I thought I was going to lose you." "Bear something strange happened to me." "You have been in a coma." "I know but I thought I heard you calling me and you brought me back to this room and then left. I don't know how but you were with me." Bear said, "That's not the half of it. There are a lot of strange things happening tonight." What do you mean?" "I don't even know how to begin to explain it myself. I can't believe that you and Sterling are friends." "Yeah, he's a pretty nice guy. Oh by the way. Those guys are behind bars and are going to be locked up for a long time." "Good." "Sam next time you tell me that you have a strange feeling about something I'm going to listen. I'm so sorry." "It's ok. I'm going to be fine."

All of a sudden the little man appeared again. Sam looked puzzled. "What's the matter Sam? Who's your friend?" Who?" "The little guy behind you." Bear turned around and there he was. "There you are. Who are you? How did you get into this room like you did? Where are you from? He answered. "Who I am is not important. The important thing is that you are ok. I'll be visiting you again soon." "What do you mean? You must have a name, what do we call you?" "If you feel like you have to call me something I guess you can call me Orb." "Ok. What are you?" "I'll answer all your questions at another time. I have to go now." "Wait, wait." "Until I see you again I want you to take this." He handed them both a two carat crystal. "This is beautiful. Thanks Orb." "It will keep you safe until my next return." Sam asked, "Safe how?" "If at any time you feel that your life is in danger, place it in your hands and it will transport you to safety. I must warn you though; you must not use it unless it is a life and death situation." The doctors and nurses were in the other room asking each other how this little guy could get into Sam's room without anyone seeing him. They knew something strange was going on. Something that they knew would never be explained.

"You were not supposed to know that we are here but because you risked your life Bear for Sam, I was able to intervene and help you. We are not able to do anything to help Earth, but from time to time we are able to intervene and help. We are only here to watch and protect you from evil ones who visit you. Just

The Emerald Ring

remember to love each other and enjoy each
day as it comes. I must go now, remember,
we'll be watching you." As fast as he popped in
he popped out.

Chapter 12: The Wedding Plans

Bear looked at Sam and smiled. "I sure do love you Sam." Sam looked at Bear, smiled back and said, "I love you bigger." Bear laughed; "I love you always and until even then." Until even then, was a line in a poem Bear had shared with her. He leaned down and kissed her. The doctor said," "You can go home in a couple of days." "I know there is so much to do. I don't know where to start." "Start by getting some rest. I am going to go on home now and I'll be back first thing in the morning." "I'll be here", said Sam. "Ok Bear, I am a little tired. See you in the morning." Bear left and Sam drifted off to sleep.

Bear left the hospital and headed for Sam's ranch. Mamie had taken Uncle Walter and Aunt Rosemary home with her. Bear knocked on the door and took a deep breath. It was the first time he had been able to let go of all the stress. Shamrock answered the door. "Come on in buddy. Your Aunt Rosemary and Uncle Walter are out on the patio." "Mamie told me she was going to bring them here for me. She sure is a gem Shamrock." "You don't have to tell me", said Shamrock. "Yeah man, what's going on with that?" "Who would have guessed, huh?" "Who would have guessed what Shamrock?" "Well I have kind of gotten to know her while I've been here and she just makes my heart jump up and down. I've never felt like this before." Kind of nice isn't it Shamrock, to have someone to share your time with you?" "Boy howdy. I've got to admit it is a lot better than hanging out with the boys." "By far", said Bear.

"Shamrock, Sam and I are getting ready to plan our wedding and there are so many things we have to decide on before we get married. Where we are going to live is one of the major decisions we're going to have to make. She did tell me that she would like to live in Oklahoma but she didn't want to have to give up her ranch." "I know Bear. this ranch means a lot to her." "Shamrock, I was wondering just how far your relationship with Mamie has gotten. I know she can count on her foreman Jake, but I don't know how much Mamie knows about running this ranch." "Well, between you and I Bear, I'll help Mamie all I can you know that. When I get enough nerve up I'm going to ask Mamie to marry me. I just don't know when yet. I know I'm not much; I am just an old truck driver." "First of all you're my best friend. My bestest buddy. Someone I would trust my life with, and at times have. So don't give me this just an old truck driver stuff. You're a good man Shamrock. Any woman would be lucky to have you." "Come on Bear." "It's true Shamrock. You're brave, not that bad to look at and a lot of fun. Come on you're a fine catch." "Ok buddy, you have convinced me." "Good that will help us in trying to figure out what to do. Sam told me that if you and Mamie were here and Jake would continue to run the ranch as a foreman, then she could live with that. Sam knows that you and Mamie wouldn't let anything happen to the ranch." "She can count on us Bear." "Great Shamrock, I can't thank you enough." "Hey that is what friends are for.

Shamrock said, "Let's go and check on Aunt Rosemary and Uncle Walter." Ok." Everything is going to be ok. Trust me Bear. Relax and take it easy for a little while. We are all here for you." Ok." Aunt Rosemary and Uncle Walter greeted Bear as he walked onto the patio. "Bear, Sam's ranch is just a real find. No wonder she is having a hard time trying to figure out where she wants to live. I just love it here. Mamie has gone out of her way to make us feel right at home. Sam is lucky to have her. "She loves Mamie very much Aunt Rosemary and believe me when I tell you that Sam has never taken her for grant it." "Bear you're a lucky man to have found her." "I know. I'm going back to the hospital first thing in the morning to be with Sam. You guys go ahead and sleep in. Aunt Rosemary I know you will find that a real treat." "I sure will. Bear you tell Sam we're here for her." "I will."

"Bear we brought Baby back with us. We didn't want to leave her there without anyone to relate to." "Good idea Aunt Rosemary. Where is Baby?" "Mamie took her to her room. Have you seen it yet?" No I haven't. Well come with me. This is something you have got to see." "Ok Bear. From what you told me it is pretty awesome." "That doesn't even begin to describe it." They reached Sam's room and they walked in. "Oh my!", said Aunt Rosemary. "What did I tell you", said Bear. "But wait, go on in." "Ok", said Aunt Rosemary. "Bear, I've never seen anything like this before, not even in magazines." "Her Grandfather had it designed and built for her when she found Baby." "Look. there is Baby. I bet she is confused. She is used to having Sam here with her at night. Here she comes. When Sam comes into her room she always comes in to meet her." Bear called to her, "Hi Baby." Baby jumped on him. Bear played with her for a few minutes. "I think I'll call the hospital to see if Sam is still asleep. Maybe if she is awake she can talk to Baby a minute." "Good idea Bear."

The phone rings in Sam's room and the nurse picked up the phone. Bear asked the nurse if Sam was awake. The nurse told him that she is taking her vital signs. "Would it be ok if I talk to her a few minutes?" "Sure I don't see why not." "Hi Sam, guess what? I have a friend of yours here that sure would like to hear your voice." "Who Bear?" "Baby. Baby is right here at the ranch. Aunt Rosemary and Uncle Walter brought her with them when they flew up here to see you." "Tell Rosemary how much I appreciate her help with Baby. I can't tell you how much it means to me." "I know Sam and I know she understands, that's why she brought her along. Ok Sam I'm putting the phone to her ear." "Hi Baby girl, how you doing? I'll be there soon ok? You be a good girl. I love you Baby." Baby looked up at Bear as if she was trying to thank him. Bear got back on the phone. "I'll let you get back to resting now. I will see you first thing in the morning. I love you." "I love you too Bear. Everything is going to be ok Stuff." That made Sam smile.

Rosemary said "Look Bear, she seems more relaxed already." Bear said, "Good girl." Mamie walked in and began showing everyone to their rooms so they could go get ready for bed. Mamie said "It's been a long day." Aunt Rosemary said it sure has. Mamie placed

The Emerald Ring

Uncle Walter and Aunt Rosemary in Sam's
Grandfathers room. Shamrock already had a
guest bedroom. "Now for you Bear." "Mamie I
have a place to go to." "I was hoping you would
stay here tonight with Baby in Sam's room. I
think Sam would like that." "Oh ok Mamie."

"Now that we have that taken care of that
does anyone want some coffee?" Bear said "I'll
have a cup Mamie." Shamrock said "Me too."
Off to the kitchen they went. "Guess what I
have Bear", said Mamie. "Wait a minute. Let
me guess." Bear smells the air.

"I know Mamie, it's a blackberry cobbler."
"Why yes it is, how did you guess that?"
"Remember Mamie I have Indian blood in me
and I can even smell anyone that has been
here in the last 24 hours." "Really?" "Wait a
minute. Jim has been here." "Yes, he was here
early this afternoon." "That is amazing Bear."
"Ok Mamie, now where is that cobbler?"
"Coming right up Bear." "What about me
Mamie?" "You can have some too Shamrock.
You poor baby." Bear said, "Yeah you poor
baby." "Ok Bear, knock it off." Mamie handed
them their coffee. "This is so good Mamie!"
Mamie told them that Sam will get to come
home in a couple of days. "That's what the
doctor", said Mamie. "That's good because

we've got a wedding to plan. I'm glad your Aunt and Uncle are here so that they can help us plan for it. I know Aunt Rosemary is eager to pitch in and help." Mamie said, "That's great Bear, because you are not giving us much time." "I don't want to waste one minute. I want her to marry me as soon as we can make it happen." "Do you guys know where you want to get married?" "No, not yet."

"Do you guys know where you want to live?" Sam told me that she would like to live in Oklahoma, but she didn't want to give up the ranch. I know she sure would miss you Mamie unless you want to live with us and I think that would be great." "I bet you do Bear", Shamrock puts in his two cents. "Wait a minute there." "What Shamrock?" "Well, I think Mamie should stay here and help with the ranch. I don't know how to run a ranch Shamrock. Jake does and I can help you, that way Sam still has the ranch. Besides that Mamie, I don't want you to leave." "You don't Shamrock?" "No, I don't." Bear laughed and shook his head. Bear said, "Well think about it Mamie and we can decide later."

"Now", said Bear, "let's get to the business at hand. Our Wedding." "What do you want to do Bear?" Just get us married. Hopefully in a church. We did agree on that." "I'm glad you

The Emerald Ring

both decided to be married in the church."
"Mamie, I asked Sterling to be my best man
and he agreed." "Good for you Bear."
Shamrock said ,"What about me Bear?" "I'm
your best friend." "I know Shamrock; it just
seemed like the right thing to do at the time."
"It's my Wedding and I can have two best
men." "No Bear, that's ok." "No Shamrock. You
are my best friend and buddy. I can't get
married without you next to me. We'll work it
out." "Ok Bear. We can't do anything until you
guys decide where you're going to get
married." "I know that would help move things
along. When I see her in the morning we'll try
to figure out where we want to get married."
"Bear I saw an advertisement on TV that said
you can go online and pick out a wedding
dress. Sam could be shopping for a dress
while she is in the hospital." "Good thinking
Mamie." "All we have to do is get her a
computer set up in her room. Bear said "I can
handle that." "We'll donate it to the hospital
when we are done."

"I am starting to feel so much better now
that we are actually in the planning process of
the wedding." "It's all going to come together
Bear. Just be patient." "I'm trying."

Bear headed off to Sam's room. Shamrock

203

stayed with Mamie and she got him another cup of coffee. "So you don't want me to go live with Sam and Bear?" "No Mamie. I don't. I'm afraid I have grown quite fond of you and I would miss you terribly." "Go on", said Mamie. "Its true", said Shamrock. "So what you're telling me is that you would be willing to stay here on the ranch and help me run it for Sam?" "You betcha!" "Tell you what. I'll give it some deep thought." "Now Mamie you know you would miss me if you went to live with Bear and Sam." "I would but you would come and see us." "That wouldn't be the same; I want you all to myself." "You do huh?"

Back in Sam's room Bear was playing with Baby and getting to know her a little better. Bear told Baby, "Baby I think Sam is in for a surprise when she gets home. You my girl are pregnant. Sam is going to be so happy. If I know my Aunt Rosemary she is going to want one of your babies." I'll call Jim first thing in the morning and have him check you out. He might be able to tell me before I leave for the hospital. I know you are but we need him to confirm it for everybody else. Good girl, Baby. I guess we had better get some sleep."

Bear got into bed and patted the bed like Sam always did and Baby jumped up with him.

The Emerald Ring

They drifted off to sleep.

Shamrock walked Mamie to her room. Mamie started to walk in and Shamrock pulled her back to him. Mamie said, "Shamrock." Shamrock planted a great big kiss on her and told her, "See you in the morning." Mamie went on into her room. Shamrock went to his room. Shamrock thinks to himself, *so far so good.*

Mamie was thinking to herself, *I can't believe Shamrock kissed me. I thought he was just clowning around because he had to stay here for a while. Imagine that. Well, I guess I had better do some serious thinking. I really like Shamrock but I never dreamed of anything being able to come out of it. I'm not going to jump into anything just because of the situation.* Mamie got ready for bed and decided to sleep on it.

Back in Shamrock's room we find him all shook up. How is he going to convince Mamie to stay on the ranch and not go live with Sam and Bear. *What am I going to do? How do I tell her that I've had more fun and enjoyed life more than any other time in my life; being here with her the last couple of weeks? I don't want to give that up. Now that I finally understand what it means to share your life with someone and I might lose it.*

Morning came and Mamie was in the kitchen making coffee and getting ready to start breakfast when Aunt Rosemary came in. "Hi Mamie. Can I help you with something?" "No you just sit a spell and enjoy. We'll have a cup of coffee before everyone gets up and around." "Sounds good to me Mamie. It sure is a beautiful morning Rosemary." "It sure is. I miss Sam. I'm usually making her breakfast by now. She is my pride and joy that girl." "You must be awful proud of her says Aunt Rosemary." "I sure am."

Mamie said, "Bear is good for her. I think they make a good couple." "Bear needs someone like Sam in his life says Aunt Rosemary." "They've always got us to fall back on." "They will be ok." Mamie laughed, we just have to get them to the alter." Rosemary agrees. "The sooner the better."

Bear walked in. "Mamie I smelled your coffee. A perfect alarm clock." "Maybe but not a permanent one." "Does that mean that you have decided to stay here on the ranch for Sam?" "No. It just means that I am not an alarm clock." Bear laughed.

"Aunt Rosemary, I asked Mamie if she

The Emerald Ring

would like to live with Sam and I after we get married." "Do you know where you are going to live yet?" No. We might stay here on the ranch and if we do she can stay here with us or if we go to Oklahoma she is welcome to come with us. I have lots of room on the ranch." "Aunt Rosemary said, "We sure do Mamie and we would have so much fun." I told him I would think about it." "Great", said Aunt Rosemary.

In walked Uncle Walter. "Coffee ready?" "Sure is Hun", says Rosemary. "Get me a cup." Rosemary got him a cup of coffee. Mamie said, "One more to go." Shamrock was still not up yet. Mamie said, "I'll start breakfast and Bear, you can go get Shamrock." "Ok Mamie, be back in a minute." "Ok".

Bear went to Shamrocks room and found him sitting on the side of the bed. "Shamrock what's wrong?" "Nothing." Bear said, "Nothing? This is Bear." "Oh alright. I've been thinking about Mamie all night. Bear what if she goes to live with you in Oklahoma." "Shamrock, I didn't know that this meant so much to you." "I didn't either until you asked her to go with you guys." "I see. Shamrock, I promise you it will be ok. I won't let you down. Ok?" "Ok buddy", said Shamrock. "Now... Mamie is cooking breakfast so we had better get to the kitchen."

Bear and Shamrock headed for the kitchen. Mamie asked Bear, "How do you want your eggs?" "Over easy Mamie." They'll be ready in a minute Bear. There you go." "I know what you want Shamrock." "Good girl Mamie". Shamrock winked at her. Mamie smiled and fixes his eggs. Shamrock said, "Mamie you're the best." Why, because I fix you good eggs?" "No because you're special." Bear chimed in and said, "You sure are Mamie. You know if Sam and I move to Oklahoma maybe I should have you stay here and take care of Shamrock for me. He needs someone to take care of him. He's been living alone for too long." "Mamie says you think so?"

There was a knock at the door. Mamie answered the door. "Jim, what are you doing here?" "Bear asked me to come and check on Baby." "I thought you did that the other day." "I did but it seems that something else has been brought to my attention." "Oh, ok." "I'll go and check on her." Bear said, "I'll come with you. Great!

"What's going on?" "You'll find out in a minute Mamie." Uncle Walter said, "I hope Baby is ok." "I'm sure she is, Bear didn't seem worried", said Shamrock. "I can't imagine what it could be, but it must have been important

The Emerald Ring

enough for Bear to call Jim", said Mamie. "I know", said Aunt Rosemary. "Sam sure does love that Cougar." "Jim and Bear come into the kitchen." Mamie said, "Well?" "Are you ready for this Mamie?" "I don't know. Do I need to sit down? Jim says might not be a bad idea." Mamie asked Jim, "Do you want a cup of coffee before I sit down?" "Sure." Mamie got him his coffee and sat down. "Bear why don't you tell them." "Ok." "Baby is going to be a Mommy." "What?" "Baby is pregnant." "Oh my goodness", said Mamie. "Sam is going to be so surprised." Bear said, "That's why I called Jim to come out here this morning so I could get him to verify it before I go to see Sam. I wanted to be able to tell her. Aunt Rosemary asked, "Do you think she will let me have one of the cubs? Bear, you know I would take good care of it." "I know but you're going to have to ask Sam about that." "Ok I will. This is great! baby cubs. I can't wait 'till she has them. This is so exciting." Bear said, "I know Aunt Rosemary but let's not forget about my wedding. I want you to get excited about that right now." "I know Bear and I am excited about it. As soon as you and Sam tell us where you want to get married we'll get right on it." "I hope to settle that this morning. Ok, I'm off to the hospital. See you guys later."

Bear left and headed for the hospital. He couldn't wait to tell Sam about Baby. Bear parked his truck and entered the hospital. He pushed the button for the elevator. The doors open up and he gets in. He over heard some nurses talking about the strange things going on in I.C.U. "Tameka said she knows that man didn't pass her to go into that ladies room. He had to go in through the door by the desk. That is the only way in. So how did he get in there?" "I don't know." The elevator door opened and they got out. Bear was thinking to himself; *If they only knew.* Bear got off on Sam's floor and headed for her room. He peeked in and said, "Hi Sam!" "It's ok come on in Bear." He leaned down and gave her a kiss. "How are you feeling this morning Sam?" "A lot better." "Good. I have a surprise for you." "What is it Bear? When Aunt Rosemary and Uncle Walter flew in they brought Baby back with them." "Oh, thank goodness. She would have been lost without someone she knew there." "That is what Aunt Rosemary said. this morning I had Jim come and check her out before I came here. How is she doing?" "Great! Are you ready for this?" "For what?" "Baby is going to be a Mommy." Bear says, "I guess the trip to the Zoo to see her friend was a visit she'll remember for awhile." "Wow, Bear baby cubs!"

The Emerald Ring

"This is totally amazing." "I know. "

"Stuff we have something else to concentrate on." "I know it's our wedding right?" "Bear I bet you are driving everybody crazy with this wedding." At that moment the maintenance men brought in a computer and started hooking it up. "Sam we have to decide on where we are going to get married before we can do any planning." Sam said, "I guess that would help huh? What do you think Bear?" "Where do you want to get married?" "I don't care as long as we hurry up and get it finalized. I don't want to spend one more day without you being my wife." "Bear, Bear." I don't care. I almost lost you once and you are very precious to me Sam." "I'm sorry Bear." "I was just teasing." I know Sam. I want our wedding to be special." "Me too", said Sam. "Ok then."

The maintenance men told Bear that the computer was all ready. "Bear, what do they mean all ready? All ready for what?" "Sam, since you can't get out and shop for a wedding dress, I thought I would bring them to you." "How?" "Mamie told me that you could go on the internet and find anything. So I thought you could probably pull up wedding dresses. Find the one you want and have it delivered."

"Oh, I see. Just like that." "Yeah", said

Bear. Why not?" Sam said, "Yeah why not", and started laughing. "What's so funny?" "Nothing Bear its ok." "No Sam. What's wrong?" "Well it's not exactly what I had in mind." "What?" "Shopping on the internet for a wedding dress."

"Sam, I'm so sorry. Look at me. I'm so wrapped up in hurrying up this wedding that I'm taking the romance out of it for you. Please forgive me." "It's ok Bear." "No it's not. Tell you what. I'll take a look on the internet and if I see something I like, Mamie and Rosemary can take me to look at it." "Are you sure Sam? "I'm sure Bear. Now you go." "I want to rest a little while." "Ok Stuff, I love you." "I love you too." "Bear., would you mind very much if we got married here?" "No that would be fine. I don't care as long as we get married. See Sam another decision made. It's moving right along."

The nurse came in to take her vital signs and Bear left. The nurse told Sam, "You sure have a handsome fellow." "Thanks! He sure is. He is a one of a kind and I'm glad he is all mine. We're getting married in a couple of weeks." "Congratulations." "Thank you." "What kind of wedding are you having?" "I don't know yet. Maybe after I look at a few wedding dresses it will come to me." Have fun." The

The Emerald Ring

nurse left the room.

Sam closed her eyes while thinking, *What kind of wedding do I want?* She drifted off to sleep. She started dreaming about the wedding. *She saw white columns with sheers flowing in the background. There was an aisle with lit palm trees on each side and flower petals leading up to the stairway to the columns. Sam was thinking to herself in her dream, if I didn't know any better I would think I was in Mt Olympus. I have to be dreaming. Everything is so beautiful.*

The phone rings and wakes her up. It was Sterling. "Hi Sam, I hope I didn't wake you up." "I was asleep but that's ok. I'm glad you called Sterling." "You are?" "Of course I am." "I thought I would come over and see you today if it is ok with you." "Sure that would be great." "Ok." "I'll let you go now and I'll see you later." "Ok. "

The doctor came in to check on Sam and told her that she could go home on Thursday if she is still doing well. "Bear will be glad to hear that Doc." "I bet he will. He is a man with a mission. He wants to get married." "I know, says Sam."

Doc said, "Everybody knows." They both

laughed. "I see Bear has your computer all set up for you. I have never seen anyone so devoted to someone like he is to you. Sam you have quite a fella there." "You got that right Doc. What am I going to do with him?" "Marry him Sam." They laughed again. "I guess I'd better start looking for my wedding dress." "See you later Sam." "Bye Doc."

Sam logged onto the computer and pulled up the internet. *Ok let's see now. Here we go.* Weddings, Dresses, Options, Traditional, Old fashion, Unusual, Casual or One of a Kind. *One of a kind, let's see what happens when I click this one.* Type in a Theme. *Ok, let me type in Goddess, Hawaiian. Cool. I like these dresses. They look so soft and flowing and comfortable.* Sam clicks on to the next one. *Oh wow, I like this one. This dress is so awesome.* Sam clicks on the dress. A phone number appears. Sam wrote down the phone number. *Now I need a veil.* Sam clicks on veils. The computer showed Sam the three veils that matched the dress that she had clicked on. *Ok. I think this is the one.* Sam clicks on the veil. Sam called the number and ordered it to be delivered to the hospital. *If this looks as good as it does on the screen then I'm all set.*

In came Sterling. "Hi Sam!" "Hi Sterling."

The Emerald Ring

"You look great Sam." "Doc says I can go home Thursday." "That's wonderful. It sure is lonely not having you in my life now. You came into my life like a whirlwind and right back out. I had my life all organized and no surprises, then up you popped and turned my world upside down. Now I just don't know what to do with myself. "I'm sorry Sterling." "It's not your fault Sam. I even love the guy. We're good friends now. I'd do anything for him. Sam said, "He does have that effect on people." "I'll always be here for you Sam." "I know Sterling." "I'd better get going now. Tell Bear I said Hey and I'll talk to you later. Ok. "

Sam laid back and fell asleep again. Sam slept for a couple of hours before the nurse had to wake her up again. Sam notices some boxes on the shelf by the window. The nurse told her that they were delivered while she was sleeping. "Ok thanks." Sam walked over to see if it was the wedding dress she had ordered and it was. "I can't believe it." "What?" "This is the wedding dress I just ordered off the internet this morning. Wow that was fast." The nurse asked, "Can I see it?" "Sure. What do you think? "

"Sam this is beautiful." "Want to try it on?" "Yes but what if Bear comes in?" "We can shut the door and put a sign on it." "Ok". The nurse went to get the sign and posted it outside her door while Sam tried on the dress. Then the nurse helped her with the veil. "You look so beautiful Sam." "Thanks Shanda. I had better get this dress off before Bear comes." She took off the dress and veil and put them back in the boxes. "Now where am I going to put them so he doesn't see them?" "I know", said Shanda, "I have a big medical box we can put the boxes in." "He'll think that they are medical supplies." "Good thinking Shanda."

Sam called Mamie and told her that she had her wedding dress. "Sam how in the world did you get a wedding dress while you were in the hospital." "You told Bear to get me on the internet, remember?" "Yes, but I didn't really think that he would do that. Wait till you see it Mamie. I want you and Aunt Rosemary to come up and see it." "We're on our way." "I don't want Bear to know I have it yet ok?" "We won't say a word." "Mamie I really wanted you to go with me to pick out my dress but Bear is kind of rushing the plans." "I know. It's ok. "I hope you like it." "Baby if you like it then I will just love it." "We decided to get married here. I guess we have accomplished a lot since this morning. After you and Aunt Rosemary see the dress we will have to figure out where to have the wedding." "Great Sam. It won't take us long to get there." "The nurse just gave me some medicine that makes me sleep so wake me up when you get here." "Ok we're on our way."

Sam drifted off to sleep again. Mamie told Aunt Rosemary about the dress. "Sam wants us to come up and see it." "What are we doing standing here? Let's go." Out the door they went. Bear pulled up in his truck just as they were backing up. Aunt Rosemary told Bear, "We'll be back in a little bit. Shamrock is out on the patio." "Ok, see you guys later."

Bear headed out to the patio to be with Shamrock. "Shamrock, what do you know ole buddy? Anything going on?" "Yeah, my buddy is getting married. Have you guys made any decisions yet?" We did decide to get married here this morning." "Ok, that helps a lot," said Shamrock. "We know where, now we have to figure out a place for you to get married. It has to be a special place Shamrock. Help me find it." "Ok Bear."

"Do you know what kind of a wedding you guys want to have? Do you want to get married in a church, park, or a house on the lake? Got any ideas." "First idea I had was a church wedding." I guess I'll let Sam think on it for a few days and we can try to make a decision on that. I just want it to be perfect for her. I think I'm going to go lay down for awhile before I go back up to the hospital." Bear headed for Sam's room and laid down with Baby for awhile.

Back at the hospital Aunt Rosemary and Mamie were in Sam's room. Aunt Rosemary said, "Bless her heart, she has been through a lot the last couple of weeks." "I know", said, Mamie. The chaplain walked in and saw Mamie. "Mamie is everything alright?" "Everything is fine now Pastor ." "We did have a close call though. I almost lost her a couple of days ago. I'm glad she is out of the woods now. We have to trust God in times like these. We do not understand sometimes why things happen. All we can do is pray for God's will to be done and to praise Him. He told us in Proverbs 3:5 Trust in the Lord with all thine heart; and lean not unto thine own understanding. In all thy ways acknowledge Him and He shall direct thy paths. We just know that He is always with us. Pastor Sam is getting married in a couple of weeks. Do you think you could marry them?" "I would consider it an honor Mamie. I'll come back later. Have her call me and we'll work out the details." The Pastor left the room.

The Emerald Ring

Sam woke up and saw Aunt Rosemary and Mamie. "How long have you two been sitting there? You should have woke me up." "We have only been here a few minutes." Ok." "Well, are you guys ready for this?" "I guess so." "Mamie you see that medical box over there?" "Yes. Open it up and get the boxes out of it." "Ok." They opened up the boxes and took out the dress and veil. Aunt Rosemary and Mamie held them up. "Sam, this dress is so beautiful! However did you find it?", asked Aunt Rosemary? Mamie said, "Sammy found it on the internet." Rosemary asked, "How does it fit Sam? Have you tried it on?" "It fits perfect." Mamie says, "Well it's meant to be then."

"Ok now, where do you want to get married? Oklahoma or here?" "Bear and I decided on that this morning. We are going to get married here." "Ok", said Aunt Rosemary. "Now we know where.

Mamie told her that the pastor from their church was just here and had agreed to marry them if they would like, "So you have a pastor." Mamie said, "All we need now is the time, place, and the food." "You guys want to see me in the dress?" "Sure Sam if you are up to it." "Here, help me put it on." Mamie looked at Sam and said, "It's perfect! I wish I could have gone looking around with you to find it."

"The Doc says I can go home Thursday if I'm still doing well. We can go and look some more if you want", said Sam. Mamie said, "No we're on a roll." "Let's keep going with the flow", said Aunt Rosemary. "Bear is going to be so surprised that so much is done." "This morning he was worried about it all coming together in time", said Mamie.

"I dreamed about my wedding day this morning." "You did?" "Yeah, it was like a mixture of a Greek Goddess and Hawaiian. There were white columns with long flowing sheers between the columns. Leading up to the columns were lit palm trees on each side of the aisle leading up to the columns." "Sam that sounds incredible says Aunt Rosemary." "It sure does", said Mamie. "We could have a pig roast setting and Jake and Frank could put it all together for us." "Walter and I can help", said Aunt Rosemary. "We cook like this all the time." "Great! now all we have to do is find some lit palm trees and columns and we're good to go." "Sam, we had better be getting home. If I know the guys they are going to be getting hungry." "Ok, I'll talk to you guys later. Take my dress with you." "Ok." "I'll talk to you guys later." "Do you want us to say anything to Bear?" "If you

The Emerald Ring

want."

Aunt Rosemary and Mamie headed for home. Mamie remembered the high school had a play using columns and told Aunt Rosemary about it. Aunt Rosemary told Mamie to call the school and see if they still have any of their props. "I think the school will let us use them as long as we returned them in good shape." "Great", said Aunt Rosemary. "Now all we have to do is find some palm trees." "Right...", says Mamie. "Where in the world are we going to find palm trees?"

Mamie pulled into the drive way and they headed for the house. Mamie put on a pot of coffee. Bear heard them and went into the kitchen. "Ok guys how is my girl doing?" Is she ready to come home yet?" "She sure is Bear", said Mamie. "Bear sit down a minute", said Aunt Rosemary. "Why do you want me to sit down? Is there something wrong?" "Oh no", said Aunt Rosemary, just the opposite. "What do you mean?, asked Bear. "The wedding is all coming together." Bear said," I don't understand. Sam still has to find a dress and we have to find a pastor and ... ." "Wait a minute Bear", said Aunt Rosemary. "Ok, what? Mamie said, "Since we saw you this morning we have found a pastor and Sam has her dress and we have part of the plans worked out for the reception but you have to talk to Sam before we go any further." Bear said how did all this happen?"

"Sam ordered her dress over the internet and they delivered it this morning. It fit perfect. It is beautiful Bear." Bear said, "Sam can make anything look beautiful." "While we were at the hospital our pastor came in to see Sam and he agreed to marry you guys. So you see everything is coming together." Bear gave a big yahoo and said he had to get to the hospital.

"Bear you be careful driving to the hospital", said Aunt Rosemary. "I will." Bear kept thinking about the wedding. *I'm getting married, I'm getting married.* That's all that kept going through his mind. *I can't believe it, I'm really getting married.* Bear pulled in to the hospital parking lot and headed for Sam's room. Bear was so excited. He walked over to Sam and looks straight into her eyes. "Sam we're getting married." "I know Bear, I know." "I mean we are really getting married." "Yes, we are really getting married." "Sam you just don't know how much this means to me." Sam took Bears hands and looked into his eyes, "yes I do Bear. We have the rest of our lives ahead of us. Slow down, ok.""Ok Sam, I will. I just love you so much. It won't be long now. I can't believe you have your dress already." "I know. cool huh?"

"The doctor might let me go home tomorrow or Friday. I can go by the flower shop and order my flowers. I guess sometime next week we'll be married." "I can't wait", said Bear. "Have you got your Tux yet?" "No." "For someone who is in a hurry to get married I'd say you had better get busy. Bear, what do you think about a Hawaiian wedding?" "Awesome Sam." "Tell Aunt Rosemary and Mamie when you get home and they will know what to do." "Ok Sam, I guess I had better get going. I have a lot to do." "Yes you do." "I'll see you later Sam." "Ok Bear."

Bear called Shamrock before he left the hospital and told him to bring Uncle Walter with him and to meet him at the Tux rental place in town. Bear called Sterling and told him to meet them there too. Bear made one more phone call to Mamie and Aunt Rosemary and told them that Sam's wedding plans were a go on the Hawaiian theme. "Thanks Bear, now we can get busy." "We're on our way to order the Tuxedo's." "Great!" Mamie called the school and made the arrangements to get the props from school. "Rosemary, it's a go on the columns." "Mamie where are we going to get palm trees?" "Let's look in the phone book." "Good idea", said Rosemary. They started looking through the yellow pages. "Here is the T's. Here we go trees. It says "We have trees to fit any setting"." "We'll see says Rosemary." "Hello, we're looking for some palm trees." The nursery asks how many would you like and what kind do you need? Rosemary said, "You mean you really have palm trees?" "Why yes." "Well my nephew is getting married and we need palm trees to put down the aisle and along the tables for the reception." "I see. I think we have just what you need." "Really?, asked Rosemary. "Really. Why don't you come in and I'll be happy to show you what we have. ask for Vicky." "Great. We'll be right there." Rosemary told Mamie that the nursery said they have just what we need. "Imagine that." "Well let's go and see what they have." "Ok."

Mamie and Rosemary headed for the nursery. They walked in and saw display after display of tree settings. "This is amazing Rosemary." "I know. Look over there." "Here are some pictures of restaurants with lit palm trees in them." "That is what we need alright." Mamie said, "It sure is. Ok Mamie let's find Vicky." "Ok. There is a lady over there. Let's see if she can help us." "Yes, what can I do for

The Emerald Ring

you?" "We're looking for a lady named Vicky.
We just talked to her a little while ago." "That's
me. You are the ones looking for palm trees?"
"Yes we are. We saw your display and I think
you are going to be the answer to our prayers."
"Wonderful!" Vicky said, "Now tell me what you
have in mind and we'll make it happen." The
three put their heads together and worked out
a plan. Vicky told them that they could take
care of everything. We will deliver them and set
them all up for you. "You will?" "Of course it's
no problem. We can come out the day before
and check things out and put it all together for
you. This is going to be such an awesome
wedding. I'm glad we can be a part of it." "So
are we Vicky." They all laughed. Mamie said,
"The way things are shaping up we can have
the wedding next Saturday.""We'll talk to you
later Vicky."

Just then Vicky's husband Gerry came in
and she introduced him to Rosemary and
Mamie. They told him about the wedding.
Gerry said, "I sure would like to take pictures of
this wedding." "You do photography?" "I sure
do. Here is my card. Hodge Photography."
"Rosemary, Mamie we'll take real good care of
you. Don't you worry about a thing. "

Rosemary said, "Can you believe it

Mamie? The only thing left is the food and the music." Mamie said, "I know Frank is working on the food. We don't have to worry about that. So what do we do for the music?" "Hey", said Rosemary. "We're on a roll."

"Let's wait until we talk to Sam about the music. She may have something in mind." "Good idea Mamie." Mamie said,"I better get home and get something started for supper. Everybody will be coming in and wanting something to eat." "I know what you mean Mamie. What can I do to help?" Mamie and Rosemary arrived home and found Frank putting corn on the cob and potatoes on the grill. Steaks are seasoned and ready to cook as they order. Mamie said, "Frank what is this?" "I know you Mamie. I thought I would give you a break this evening and let you enjoy the evening for a change. You're always making sure everyone eats and you're always busy. Tonight you relax." "Thanks Frank! I really appreciate it." "Now go, go on. You and Rosemary get some ice tea, kick your shoes off and watch a movie or something." "Great! Ok."

Mamie told Rosemary, "I feel lost." "I bet you do", said Rosemary. Mamie sat in the recliner, leaned back and took a deep breath.

"This is nice. I could get used to this."

The Emerald Ring

Rosemary put a movie on, leaned back and got comfortable. They looked at each other and said at the same time, "Where's the pop corn?" They burst into laughter.

Meantime Bear and Shamrock had come home and had Frank throw on their steaks. Bear had come in to touch base with Mamie and Aunt Rosemary when he heard them laughing their hearts out. He walked in and said, "Well lookie here." "Hi", Bear said. Rosemary asked, "How long have you been here?" "We just got here a few minutes ago. Frank threw our steaks on. Are you guys ready to eat?" "Sure Bear we got a lot of things done today. The only thing to tie up now is the music."

"I have that covered Mamie", said Bear. "Great, then we're good to go", Aunt Rosemary said. "next Saturday at 5:30pm at the ranch", Bear said. "sounds like a plan to me. Now what am I going to do until then?, asked Bear. I am going to be a nervous wreck. "We know", said Mamie and Aunt Rosemary.

"Mamie, the doctor said Sam can come home Thursday morning. It will be good to have her home again." "I guess I'll spend next week at work says Bear." "Have you decided to stay on or are you guys moving to Oklahoma?"

227

"I guess that all depends on you and Shamrock, Mamie." "What does Sammy want to do Bear?" "I think she wants to go to Oklahoma." Mamie suggested to Bear, "You guys can really go back and forth." "Of course we can Mamie. We're not leaving home Mamie. You are going to see a lot of us." "I know. Now let's go eat."

"Bear here's your steak just the way you like it." "Thanks Frank. It looks so good and I'm hungry." "Mamie told me the way you like your steak." Bear said," Good ole Mamie." Ok Mamie here is yours."

"Yummy", said Mamie. "Rosemary here is yours." "Looks great Frank! Thanks." "Chow down guys." Walter and Shamrock had already started eating. "Bear, this is so good." "Wait till you taste it. The steak just melts in your mouth. It's so tender. Ahhhhh, oh man, this is good. Frank I think I love you." They all laughed. Frank said, "Well I'm glad you like It Bear because it is on the menu for your reception if it's ok with you." "Are you kidding? This is great."

After talking the menu over with Frank, Bear headed for the stable. He leaned against the fence and looked up at the stars. He was thinking to himself how lucky he was to be marrying Sam. He stood there enjoying the peace and quietness of the evening, while the night creatures stole away the silence of the night. One by one the symphony of the night began. The croaking of the frogs and the crickets begin their harmony with the clicking sound, the owls hooting and the doves cooing. Soon the dancing of lightning bugs began and he watched with anticipation, the show of the night. Bear took a big breath of fresh air and headed for the house.

Bear headed for Sam's room and calls her. "Hi Sam. I sure do miss you and I know I just saw you a couple of hours ago. "I know." "I have all our Tuxedo's ordered. Frank has the menu for the reception down pat." Totally awesome Sam. "You don't have to tell me Bear. I know how good he is." "I'm going to take care of the music tomorrow. I know someone who will be perfect for this kind of reception. Sam do you have any special music in mind?" "No Bear I think I'm going to leave this one all up to you." "Ok." Sam said, "Surprise me." "You got it."

Baby jumped up on the bed with Bear. "Sam here is Baby." Bear put the phone up to her ear. Sam talked to her for a minute. Hearing Sam's voice perked her up. "Ok Sam

I'm going to have to calm her down now and get ready for bed. I want to come and see you first thing in the morning before I go in to work." "Ok Bear, I Love you." "I love you Sam."

Sam said, "I want to tell my boss that I'm probably going to be quitting after next week. He's not going to be happy about that." I know", said Bear. "Good night Stuff. I'll see you in the morning." "Ok, night Bear."

Bear calmed Baby down and they fell asleep. After a good night's sleep Bear woke up, got ready in a hurry and headed for the hospital. He peaked in to see Sam sleeping. A nurse asked Bear if he would like a cup of coffee. "Sure that would be great." "Sam is so excited about the wedding. She was telling me about it. It sounds like an incredible wedding." "We hope so. We're putting it together one step at a time." "I'll get your coffee." Bear looked back in on Sam. *Oh Sam, I sure do love you.*

Bear noticed the computer was still in Sam's room. Bear slipped over to the computer and logged on. Bear thinks to himself, *Now let's see here. www.hawaiansinger.com. Ok now, Your old friend, Bear here…getting married… would like for you to sing at my wedding. You have my number or email reply for next Saturday 5:30PM…will understand if*

The Emerald Ring

Sam started to wake up. Bear logged off. "Morning Stuff. How's my girl?" "Your girl is ready to go home. I know Hun, I'll take you home right now if you want." "No. That's ok. It's only one more day. I just want to go home. We have to decide on where we are going to live. What did Mamie and Shamrock say?" "I think they are going to say yes." "I hope so." "Mamie said we could live in both places. Bless her heart."

"I told her that we weren't running away from home. Shamrock will take good care of her. I know he will. I'll talk to work and get some things done there." "Ok." Bear gave her a kiss and held her in his arms. "See you later Stuff."

Dr. Kennedy came in and told her that she was doing fine. "You can go home any time tomorrow. All your tests look real good and the x-rays are ok." "Dr. Kennedy, thank you for all of your help." "You know Sam it was a lot more than my help that got you this far."" I know, praise God." "Praise God and the love of that man of yours. He never gave up Sam. He believed you would come back to him. Your love for each other is like none that I have ever seen. Mamie told me you two were soul mates.

231

I believe she is right. I'll go write up your discharge orders for tomorrow. If you need anything give me a call." "Would you like to come to our wedding next Saturday?" "Sure I'd like that. I'll give your nurse the details." See you later Sam."

The phone rings it is Mamie. "Hi Mamie I'm finally coming home." Mamie said, "If I know Bear he will be there at five in the morning." "I know and I can't wait." "Has Bear been there yet?" "Yes. He had to get to work to take care of a few things. I know he is dreading telling his boss that he will probably be quitting after next Saturday. They have become good friends. So Mamie, have you and Shamrock decided on anything yet?" "Sam, if that is what you want then of course I'll stay here." "Mamie, you're still going to see us a lot." "I hope so." "We'll be flying back and forth all the time. So what are you and Aunt Rosemary doing today?" "We are going to be getting everything lined up for your wedding. I can't believe how everything has just fallen into place. I'm going to let you go Sam, so I can get some breakfast going." "Ok Mamie."

The phone rings, it was Vicky. "Hi Vicky, Gerry and I were wondering if it would be alright if we came out this afternoon to take a

The Emerald Ring

look at the area that we are going to be working with." "Sure. That will be fine. If Rosemary and I are not here, Frank will be able to help you." "Great! See you later."

Mamie started breakfast and Shamrock was the first one in the kitchen. "Shamrock, I told Sam this morning that if you staying on here and helping me run the ranch for her is what she wants then it is ok with me." Shamrock started doing a little jig, grabs Mamie and twirls her around. "Yeehaw!", shouted Shamrock. "Shamrock, behave yourself." Mamie said, "Now sit down and I'll fix you a cup of coffee. I've got to get breakfast going." "Ok Mamie."

Mamie got everyone's breakfast ready before she and Rosemary headed out to get things taken care of for the wedding. Bear was taking care of things at work. Mamie and Rosemary dropped off the wedding cake book for Sam to look through so she could pick out a cake to order. Morning and afternoon had come and gone before they knew it. They headed for home to relax for a little while.

Bear finished at work and headed for the hospital. He called ahead to have them deliver flowers for her. Just as they were delivering the flowers Bear arrived. "Hi Sam." She read the card. "Bear why did you get me flowers? I'm going home in the morning." I know. You can enjoy them tonight and you can take them home with you in the morning. "Bear, Bear, Bear, what am I going to do with you?" "I know... I'm going to marry you." "Yes, yes, yes", said Bear and they start laughing.

"Bear Mamie and Rosemary dropped off a wedding cake book for us to look through and pick out a cake." "Sam did you see any that you liked?" "Yes. I thought this one would be good, what do you think?" I like it so go ahead and order it." Sam picked up the phone and ordered the cake. "Now that's out of the way." "That takes care of everything Sam. All we have to do now is wait for Saturday." "And you were worried about the wedding Bear. See it all got planned before I even got out of the hospital." Mamie has agreed to let Shamrock stay on and help her with the ranch. "Great!" "Sam I'm going to stay here all night and as soon as you wake up we're out of here." "You can't do that." "Yes I can." "I know you think you can do anything but Baby needs you. I'll be fine and I will rest a lot easier knowing you are there with her." "Ok, but be ready because first thing in the morning you're out of here." "I'll be ready."

The Emerald Ring

Bear headed for the ranch. Mamie had put some supper back for him in case he hadn't eaten. She had also baked a blackberry cobbler and put it with his food. Bear walked into the kitchen and saw the cobbler. *Good ole Mamie.* Mamie heard him come in and went to the kitchen. "I thought I would find you in here." Bear said, "Now I know that you made this just for me, right Mamie?" She laughed and said, "Of course I did. I put back a plate from supper for you too." "Thanks Mamie. I really didn't take the time to eat today. I was trying to get things cleared up at work and then went to see Sam. I'll have her here for breakfast Mamie. First thing in the morning, I'm going after her." Mamie brought him a glass of milk for his supper and cobbler for dessert. "This sure is good Mamie." "Thanks Bear." Bear says, "Since I'm going after Sam in the morning I'd better try and get some sleep. He walked over to Mamie and gave her a hug, "Night Mamie." He passed Aunt Rosemary in the hall and told her, "Sam will be here in the morning." Rosemary headed for the kitchen. "Hi Mamie, Bear looks exhausted." "He sure does." "He said he would have Sam here for breakfast." "He probably will too. Frank said that Gerry and Vicky are coming over sometime tomorrow to get a feel of the place for the pictures." "Good, then they will be able to meet Sam and Bear. Do you want some coffee Rosemary?""No I think I'm going to turn in too." Mamie said, "I'm right behind you. See you in the morning."

Bear gave Sam a quick call. "Sam I just called to say I love you." "Thanks Bear. I love you too. Just think I'm going to be home in the morning." Bear said, "I can't wait. Remember first thing in the morning Sam." "I'll be ready." "Good night."

It seemed like Sam had just closed her eyes when she heard someone saying wake up, wake up Sam. She opened her eyes and it was Bear standing there. "What are you doing here? I thought you were coming first thing in the morning." "It is morning Sam." "What? Already? It seems like I just went to sleep." "Come on let's get ready to go home." Ok, ok give me a minute." "I already have your discharge papers and I have a wheelchair for you right here." "The nurses already know I'm here." In walked Dr. Kennedy. "Well Sam, I guess you're ready to go home. I knew Bear would be here first thing so I made sure I was going to be here to help speed things up."

"Thanks Doc." "Ok Sam, as soon as you sign these papers you're free to go." Sam signed the papers and Bear put her in the wheel chair. The nurse came in to take her downstairs. "Good luck you guys", said Dr. Kennedy. "See you Saturday." "Ok Doc, thanks for everything."

Bear puts her into the car and off they went. "Mamie is fixing you your favorite breakfast." "Good I'm starved." "Mamie will be glad to hear that." Bear pulled up into the driveway and he could smell the coffee. Mamie heard them pull up and headed straight for Sam. She gave her a big hug. "Come on in Sam. I've got your tea ready." "Thanks Mamie. I'm so hungry I could eat a ....". Mamie interrupted, "Drink your tea Sam and I'll have your breakfast ready in a second."

Bear sat down beside Sam. "You ready to eat Bear?" "I've got everything I need right here Mamie but since you're cooking." Mamie laughed, "I know." Here is a cup of coffee. Breakfast will be ready in a jiffy." Mamie brought Sam a couple of French toasts with powdered sugar, melted butter and syrup on them. "Yummy", said Sam. Mamie brought Bear some bacon, eggs, toast French toast and some hash browns with green peppers and onions. "Mamie you're the best." Just as they were finishing their breakfast Shamrock and Uncle Walter came in. "Sam, you're home." They reached down and gave her a big hug. Mamie brought them each a cup of coffee and started their breakfast.

In comes Rosemary. "Morning Rosemary", said Mamie. "How about some coffee?" "Yes, but Mamie I'll get it." Mamie handed Rosemary Shamrock and Walter's breakfast. Rosemary said, "There you go boys. Are you ready Rosemary?" "Sure, I'll have some French toast." Mamie fixed Rosemary and herself some French toast. "Here we go Rosemary." "This looks great Mamie." "Thanks." "You're welcome." They all got caught up on everything that was going on. Walter excused himself to go and help Frank with some things. Sam and Bear headed in to see Baby. Rosemary said that she was going to sit out on the front porch for awhile. Shamrock and Mamie were left in the kitchen. Mamie said, "Can I get you anything Shamrock?" "Well Mamie, I'll bet I can think of something."

"Shamrock, thank you for staying on with me here at the ranch." "I'll do anything I can to help. Mamie you do know I care a lot for you don't you? Every day you become more and more important to me. is that ok Mamie?" Yes Shamrock, you're becoming special to me too." "I'm going out to find Frank and Walter, see ya

The Emerald Ring

later." He reached over and kissed her on the forehead. Mamie smiled. Shamrock left and Mamie joined Rosemary on the porch. "Looks like the kids will be married soon. I'm glad she is marrying Bear Mamie. They sure do make a cute couple." "They are going to be just fine. They will always have us as a back up, they can't go wrong." "I know", said Rosemary. "What time is Vicky and Gerry going to be here?" "I don't know says Mamie."

"I am so glad we found them." "They will be a lot of help to us", said Rosemary. "Let's go and see where we want all of this to take place before Vicky and Gerry get here Mamie." "Ok, sounds like a plan to me as Bear would say." They laughed and off they went to find the perfect place to pull off this wedding.

"How about over here by the barn? We can put a platform in front of the barn doors and put up tables along the driveway. The palm trees can be put down the sides of the driveway." "I think we've got it Mamie. We're on a roll." Mamie said, "I think Gerry and Vicky will really make this area look like a real paradise." Rosemary said, "If they make it look like the places in the pictures we saw I'll think I'm on vacation. Let's go and have another cup of coffee Rosemary." "Good idea, they should be here soon." "I think we can relax now Mamie. There is nothing else left to figure out. Once Gerry and Vicky get here and see what they are going to do we can sit back and take it easy."

"We still have to figure out what we are going to wear Mamie. Let's go shopping after Vicky and Gerry leave. Do you think Sam and Bear would want to go with us?" "We can ask them. I think Bear would have fun watching us pick out a dress. Can you imagine the ribbing he would give us?" "I know", said Mamie. Mamie said, "Since Sam didn't get to let us help her pick out her dress I think she might like to help us." Mamie heard Bear singing in the kitchen. "Let's go and ask him says Rosemary. Ok."

"So how are you doing this morning Bear?" "I'm on cloud nine ladies. What are you two ladies up to?" "We're going shopping for our dresses for the wedding. We were wondering if you and Sam would like to go with us to pick them out." "Sure I would and I bet Sam would too." "I'll go ask her." "Ok." Bear said, "Be back in a minute."

The phone rings,. Mamie answered, "Hello." "Hello is my Mom there?" Rosemary, this is Dusty." "Mom, can I be in Bears

The Emerald Ring

Wedding?" "Sure Dusty, I don't think he would mind. I'll ask him." Bear walked in and Rosemary told Bear that Dusty was on the phone. "Hey Dusty. What's up?" "I was wondering if I could be in your wedding." "Sure I think that would be great! You can be one of my Groomsmen." "Yahoo" said Dusty."

"I'll have your Mom make all the arrangements for you. I'll see you soon ok?" "Do you want to talk to your Mom now?" "Tell her I'll talk to her later." "Bye." "Well ladies, Sam is all excited about our shopping trip." "Great." Bear asked, "so when do we go?" "We can go as soon as Gerry and Vicky leave." "Who is Gerry and Vicky?" "We met them at the place where we found the palm trees for your reception. I'm glad the two of you are going to be here so you can meet them and work out the details. Bear, we not only found someone who can help with the reception, but can also take your wedding pictures." "What a break", said Bear. "I can't wait to meet them." "Come with us and we'll show you where we think a good place for the wedding and the reception would be. I guess if you two wanted to be married in the church and have the reception here we could do that too. Whatever you decide is fine with us. Look. There is Gerry and Vicky. Bear go get Sam." "Ok." "Be back in a minute."

Mamie and Rosemary walked over to greet them. "Hi, we're glad you could come and take a look around before the big day.

"You sure do have a nice place here." "Oh, it's not mine. It belongs to Sam." "Well it is still a nice place." "Rosemary and I thought this area would make a good set up for the wedding and reception." "The trees can line the driveway to the barn. We can build a platform for them to walk up to for the wedding ceremony. Vicky said, "That sounds like it will work. We'll get it all set up the night before so if there are any problems we can fix them." Sam and Bear walked up and Rosemary introduced them to Vicky and Gerry. "Very nice to meet you", said Gerry and Vicky. "Rosemary and Mamie told me a little bit about the wedding but if you could fill me in on what you have in mind I'll do my best to make it all come together." Rosemary and Mamie headed back to the house while Sam and Bear spoke with Gerry and Vicky.

Mamie and Rosemary got dressed to go shopping. They waited for Sam and Bear on the porch swing. Walter walked up from the barn. "What are you two ladies up to?" "We thought we would go into town to get our dresses for the wedding." "Good luck and have fun shopping." "Frank and I are going fishing. See you guys when you get back." Gerry and Vicky left and Sam and Bear asked the ladies if they were ready to go. "We're as ready as we will ever be", said Mamie. "Let's go", said Bear. Away they went.

At the dress shop Bear was having a ball. Whistling at the ladies as they tried on their dresses. Needless to say the women were embarrassed. Mamie told Bear, stop teasing like that. "You can't do that in a store like this." "Sure I can Mamie." "Ok Sam, which one do you like out of all we have tried on?" "It's up to you. I want you to wear something comfortable. Get whichever one you like and are the most comfortable in." Mamie and Rosemary picked out the ones they liked best and they were off for home again. Mamie said, "I'm glad that is over with. Lunch time guys." "Where do you want to eat?" "We don't care Bear." "Anywhere." "Do you want to go through a drive through or go somewhere to sit down to eat." "Mamie said I would rather get it to go." "Me too", said Rosemary. "I want to go home and kick my feet up a minute and relax." "Sounds like a plan to me", said Bear. They drove up to a McDonald's drive thru and then they were good to go.

Mamie and Rosemary were stuffed, so when they get to the ranch they kicked off their shoes and sat for awhile. "I sure had a lot of fun Rosemary." "I did too Mamie. Bear laughed so hard I thought he was going to end up rolling on the floor." Sam came in and asked what was so funny? "I wish we could do this more often. I think we should leave the Bear home next time though." They all laughed and agreed that was a good idea.

The phone rings, it is Vicky. "Hi Vicky", said Mamie. "Is everything working out ok?" "I have it all laid out and ready for their approval." "Great, that didn't take very long." "I can bring the layout there or you can come in and take a look at it." "I'll tell Bear and see what he says and get back to you." "Great!"

The next couple of days went by very quickly even though Bear thought it was taking forever. Thursday morning Rosemary had to pick up Dusty at the airport. "He's all excited about Bears Wedding. Rosemary, do you want me to go with you to pick up Dusty?" "No, that's ok. Bear and Walter said they would go get him." "I'm anxious to meet him. He sounds like a very nice young man." "He is and all the girls think he is quite the hunk. I think that is how they say it today. I don't know about these kids." "Rosemary, what is Dusty's favorite food? I want to fix him something he likes to make him feel welcome." "Mamie you cook it and it is his favorite food. That boy loves to eat." "Let's cook out tonight." "Good idea Mamie."

Mamie went to find Frank and asked him if he would mind grilling up some steaks tonight. "Sounds great Mamie." "Walter and Bear went to pick up Rosemary's son from the airport. They should be back soon." "I'll get right on it Mamie." "Rosemary and I will fix up some things too." Rosemary and Mamie put together some slaw, potato salad and some baked beans.

"I hear the guys Mamie." Rosemary went to greet her son Dusty. "How was your trip Dusty?" "It was great Mom." "How is Sam doing?" "She is going to be fine Dusty." "I was worried about her." "Come on in and see for yourself." "Ok." Dusty hurried over to Sam and gave her a real big hug. "Sam, I am so glad to see that you are going to be ok." So what is this about you wanting to be in our wedding?" "Can I Sam?" "Of course you can Dusty. I think your Mom has already ordered your Tuxedo." "Wow that's great." Mamie asked Dusty to go with her and she would show him where he could put his things. "Ok Mamie."

Dusty got all settled in and Bear showed him around the ranch. Bear took Dusty to see Sam's horse Star. I sure would like to ride him Bear." "I don't think that is going to be possible Dusty. Sam is the only one who can ride Star. Star won't let anyone ride him but Sam." "That's pretty cool though Bear. Imagine having a horse that no one else can ride but you. Wow." "Dusty if you think that is cool wait until you see what I am going to show you next."

Bear and Dusty headed for Sam's room. "Dusty when we go into Sam's room I want you to stay calm." "Ok". "What is in there?" "Sam has a pet cougar." "A cougar?", asked Dusty in a slightly raised voice.

"The cougars name is Baby. We don't want to get her excited right now because she is pregnant. She won't hurt you at least as long as Sam and I are with her." "Do you think she will like me Bear?" "I don't know. We'll find out in a minute." Bear and Dusty walked into Sam's room and out came Baby. Baby walked over to Bear. Baby looked at Dusty and sniffed him and then just sat there looking at him. Bear introduced Baby to Dusty and he reached out to pet her. Dusty started to scratch her behind the ears. "Baby loves that. I think she likes

you." "Alright", says Dusty. "Let's go find Sam."
"Ok."

"Dusty I've heard a lot about you." Dusty said, "All good I hope. I just love your cougar." "Thanks. I think she likes you too." "Are you and Bear going to live here or in Oklahoma?" "We're going to live in Oklahoma. "Are you going to bring Baby with you?" "Of course, she is my baby. You are going to be seeing a lot of her." "Wow this is so awesome."

"Let's go and have some lunch. Mamie told me that Frank is grilling some steaks tonight. "

After lunch Bear gave Gerry and Vicky a call to invite them over for the Bar-b-que. Gerry said, "Sure, we'd love to come but our niece is here visiting. Can we bring her?" "Sure that's fine." "Great, see you then."

"Dusty there is a young lady coming to the bar-b-que tonight. You will have someone your own age to talk to. You won't have to hang around us old folks." "I like you old folks, but you did say it is a young lady, right?" "Dusty be nice", said Rosemary. "I will Mom." "Dusty is quite the ladies man back home." "I can't help it Mom." "I know it's your natural charm. I inherited it from Bear."

Walter took Dusty out to the barn to find

Frank and introduce him. "Hi Frank, this is my son Dusty." "Nice to meet you Dusty. How do you like your steak?" "Medium well." "You got it. How do you like the ranch Dusty?" "It's great. I see why Sam will miss it. Bear told Sam that he would fly her back and forth a lot so it won't be too bad." Frank said, "This is the only home she has ever known. It is a part of her Grandfather and now it is a part of her. It is more than just a ranch to her."

Walter and Dusty headed back to the house. Mamie asked, "Can I fix you guys something to drink?" "Some ice tea would be great Mamie." "Coming right up." In walked Shamrock. "Hi Shamrock", said Dusty. "What are you doing here Dusty?" "I am going to be in Bears Wedding." "Alright!" "Would you like something to drink Shamrock", asked Mamie? "Sure. I'll have some tea." "Ok."

"I can't believe that in two days Sam and Bear will be married." "I know", said Shamrock. "We are on a countdown now. He is going to make a lot of women unhappy. We can't forget about all those men that have been chasing after Sam too. We should call Sterling and see if he would like to come tonight. "I know it is short notice but he may come.

"Gerry, Vicky and their niece should be

The Emerald Ring

here within the next two hours." "What does she look like Mamie?", asked Dusty. Mamie told Dusty that she had never met her. "You will know soon enough. She is visiting from out of town."

Rosemary told Mamie I guess it's about time to get this dinner going. Walter told Rosemary that he was going to see if Frank needed any help. Mamie told Rosemary, "I think we have everything under control here. We should go and sit a spell." "Sounds good to me." They went into the living room and propped up their feet. Mamie and Rosemary fell asleep while watching an old movie. The door bell rung and woke them up.

It was Gerry and Vicky with their niece. Mamie answered the door. "Come on in and make yourself at home." "Mamie, Rosemary this is our niece Tara." "Welcome Tara. I hope you have a nice time this evening. Bears nephew flew in today for the wedding." "Gerry says, see Tara you won't be the only young person here." Just about that time in walked Dusty. Mamie introduces Tara to Dusty. "Dusty told Tara, "I'm really glad you could come. I hope you like steak because from what I hear Frank grills up an awesome steak. "

Sam and Bear came in. Gerry introduced

Tara to them. Bear told Tara that she is a very
pretty young lady. "Thanks", said Tara. "Watch
out for Dusty." "Thanks a lot Bear", said Dusty.
"No, he's ok. I like to tease him a lot." "I see",
said Tara. "Tara, do you like horses?" "Yes I
do." "Would you like to see some?" "Ok." Gerry
said, "They will be fine. Bear take everyone out
to the patio and we will bring everything out
there. "

"You need any help?" Rosemary told Bear,
"No thanks we got it." Frank and Walter had
already started the steaks. Sam had put on
some music to make it seem more like a party.

Rosemary took a look out the kitchen
window and saw Dusty and Tara. "Dusty seems
to be quite smitten with Tara." "You think so
Rosemary?" "Look Mamie. What do you think?"
"I think you're right. It is usually the young
ladies that are falling all over Dusty but he
seems to be the one falling all over her. Now
the shoe is on the other foot Mamie. The next
few days should be interesting." They laughed.

"Here they come, let's go back to the Patio.
"Your steak is ready Dusty", said Frank. "Is
your friend ready for one too?" "Are you ready
to eat Tara?" "Sure tell Frank how you like your
†eak." "Medium well please." "You got it. Here
ᑀe right here." "Great." Tara took her plate

over to where Dusty was sitting.

Sam started telling Vicky about her dream of the wedding. "Wow, that sounds awesome Sam. We'll do our best to make it work. Gerry and I will start putting it all together tomorrow." "Do you really think you can?" "Sure I don't see why not. Mamie and Rosemary have already done their part." "What's that?" "Finding the columns, all we have to do now is bring it all to the same place and piece it together. Piece of cake!" "Ok if you say so Vicky." Bear asked Sam to dance with him. Tara told Dusty that Sam and Bear sure seem to be in love. Dusty said that when they find the definition to love, it will read Sam and Bear. Tara said, "Why Dusty that is so sweet." Dusty said, "I want to be just like Bear." Dusty asked Tara, "You are coming to the wedding aren't you?" "Of course I am." Dusty said, "This wedding is getting better every minute."

Gerry and Vicky bid them good night. "Tara it is time to go. We have a lot to do tomorrow to get this wedding ready." "Ok, I'm ready. I guess I'll see you some time tomorrow Dusty." "Ok see you tomorrow."

While finishing up the breakfast dishes Mamie heard activity going on outside. She peeked out the window and saw Gerry, Vicky,

251

and their crew. They had already started getting things set up for the wedding. Gerry had a long trailer with the columns from the school on it.

Walter and Shamrock had already started building the platform for the columns. Frank was busy getting the electricity running for the lighting. Uncle Don drove up with a truck full of tables to go up and down the driveway. After a couple of hours it all started to come together. Mamie, Rosemary, Sam and Bear were amazed at how everything was falling into place.

Bear would get the music lined up after everyone was finished. It all looked like it was out of a fairy tale book. Everything had a romantic setting. Tara and Dusty had just finished decorating the dance floor. They all stepped back to take a look at what they had done. Gerry and Vicky both agreed that this was the most beautiful setting that they had ever been involved in creating.

Bears cell phone rings. It was the famous Hawaiian singer. Hey buddy. I'm all settled in and ready for you. Bear said, "Great!" "I'll hook up with you in about an hour." "You got it Bear. I'll kick back in my room until you get here." "I can't believe that you found the time to come."

The Emerald Ring

"Are you kidding? I had to move a few things around but I wouldn't miss this for anything. I'll let you go for now and I will see you shortly." "Bye."

Gerry asked Tara if she was ready to go. "I guess so. Vicky told her that they would be back tomorrow night for the wedding. "Sam, Bear thank you for letting me come to your wedding. I can't wait to see you two get married." Bear said, "It won't be long now. Just think Sam, tomorrow night you are going to be my wife." "Bear do you think after that we might be able to slow down a little?" They all laughed. "Ok, let's go." "We'll see you all tomorrow." They all say good night.

"Sam, do you want to walk me to my truck?" "I can't see you from now until the wedding, bad luck." "Sam I can't wait until I see you walking down the aisle. You'll be walking towards me, the luckiest man in the world." They embraced each other and kissed good night. "Tell the guys I'll pick up our Tuxedo's and take them to Uncle Don's in the morning." "I'll meet you tomorrow at the end of the aisle Bear." "Bear said, "It's a date."

Everyone got ready for bed and rested for the big day tomorrow. Mamie went into Sam's room. They spent some time together before things started to get hectic. "Tomorrow is a big day Sam. Mamie, there are no words that can express how much I appreciate you and all that you have done for me.

I love you so much Mamie." "Sam, that says it all right there. I love you too Sam. You are the little girl I never had. I think Bear is going to make you a fine husband. He'll take good care of you Sam. "I know I don't have to worry as long as you are with Bear. He sure is protective isn't he?"

"Sam are you sure that Bear is the one you want to marry?" "I'm sure Mamie." "I know Sterling loves you too." "I know but it's not the same with Sterling." The phone rings and it is Sterling. "Mamie and I were just talking about you." "How about that." "I'm glad you called Sterling." "You are Sam." "Of course I am." "Are you going to be at the wedding tomorrow?" "No Sam. I think that would be hard for me." "I understand." "Bear told me that he is doing a video of the wedding and he would make me a copy if I wanted. Know in your heart that I am with you Sam."All I want is for you to be happy. It just wasn't my time but who knows, maybe someday. I'm going to let you go. You have to rest up for your big day."

"Mamie that was Sterling. He said he can't

make it tomorrow." "I thought it might be hard on him. Let me get out of here and let you rest up for tomorrow." "Good night Mamie."

Chapter 13: The Wedding

Mamie woke up thinking *my little girl will be leaving me today. I know it will be ok though. This is a good day. Shamrock will be here with me. That will help me a lot. I sure am going to miss her. I guess I had better get up and get this day started. Everybody is going to be looking for coffee. I think it might be a good idea to put on the big coffee pot.*

Sam woke up and Baby started licking her on the arm. "I know Baby. I sure am going to miss you. Rosemary said she would watch you while Bear and I go on our honeymoon. Rosemary loves you and I know she will take real good care of you. Right now you need all the TLC you can get being pregnant. I know the Zoo would take good care of you but not like Rosemary will. Bear and I will be back before you know it. I guess I had better get this show on the road." Sam got dressed and headed for the kitchen.

"Morning Sam." "Morning Mamie, I see you got out the big pot this morning. Good thinking Mamie." Walter came into the kitchen. "How about a cup of coffee?"

"Here you go", said Mamie. Shamrock

smelled the coffee and headed for the kitchen. He came through the door and Mamie handed him his cup of coffee. "Thanks Mamie." "I knew you were on the way. Before I forget, Bear wanted me to tell you that he is picking up your Tuxedo for you." Walter is Rosemary alright?" "I better go check on her." The phone rings.

"Hi sweetheart, how is my new wife to be? Ready to get married? It won't be long now." "Are you coming out?" "No back luck, I'm not taking any chances. I'll be there around 3:30. I'm having the Tux's sent over for the guys. I sure do love you." "I love you too Bear." "Meet you at the Altar." "Sam said, "I won't be late."

Mamie and Rosemary got ready to do some finishing touches on the house and the guys went out to get more wood for the bonfire. Shamrock said, "I can't believe how Gerry and Vicky have turned this place into a real paradise." "Incredible says Walter." "I saw Bear working on something yesterday but I don't know what it is. He said it is a surprise for Sam. No telling what that could be." "I know says Shamrock. I'm going to give him a call." "Hey Bear how's things going?" Everything here is all ready." Bear told Shamrock the music was all taken care of. "The musicians should be arriving soon. I told them I would be there

around 3:30." "Who is coming Bear?"
Remember the most famous Hawaiian singer
in the world?" "Yeah, he is coming?" "He sure
is. He is bringing his band, wife and kids."

   "Bear is there anyone you haven't helped
somewhere?" "Sure there is. I was just in the
right place at the right time, that's all." "Bear I
know the things you do to help people may not
seem like anything to you, but it does help
make a difference in their lives. It means a lot
to them." "When they get here take them in to
see Mamie and she will make them feel right at
home." "You got it Bear. Mamie said Sterling
called this morning and said he isn't going to
be able to make it so I guess it is just me for
your Best Man." "That'll work Don and I will be
there in about an hour." "Count down Bear."
"Clocks ticking", said Bear. "Here comes Uncle
Don and Bobbie. I have a couple of guys from
the police department to help with parking the
guest cars." "Good. I didn't think of that." "I
gave the Tux to Uncle Don to bring out here.
So you guys are all set. See you shortly."

   Frank started the bonfire to get some hot
coals going. "That will help keep the fire going
later." Bears friends from the plice department
arrived and Shamrock showed them where the
guests could park. It seemed like minutes

The Emerald Ring

when the guests started arriving. "If you have any trouble, get a hold of Frank or me." "We won't have any trouble."

Uncle Don and Bobbie were already dressed. Shamrock and Walter went in to get dressed for the wedding. Rosemary had started getting ready too. Mamie had just finished washing and getting ready when Frank brought in George and his family. The band went over to get the stage all set up. Shamrock got ready and headed for the kitchen to tell Mamie about George when she saw him and his family. "George, how long have you been here?" "I just got here." "Great, Bear wanted me to introduce you to Mamie. She is going to be the lady of the house now after Sam and Bear get married. Mamie that is George and his family. Bear asked George to sing at the wedding." "So you're a singer?" "Well I try." "George is the best singer ever Mamie." "We're lucky to have him here." "Well set yourself down." "Make yourself at home. If you see something you want let me know or if I don't have it I'll try to get it for you." "That's ok Mamie." "Are you hungry?" "I'll fix you something to eat. How about you kids? Kids are always hungry." "No thank you we're fine Mam." "How about something to drink? We have ice tea, coffee, punch, and soda." "Ice tea would be fine Mamie." "Thanks." Shamrock, took them out on the patio. Bear came in and asked if George had arrived yet? "Yes. He's on the patio." "Now Bear, you should go get ready." "He is trying to keep from seeing Sam before the wedding." "Good ole Bear, trying to follow tradition." "Mamie is Sam in there?" "No you're safe." "Ok. Hey George ole buddy, I have to go and get ready. See you later." "Great Bear. So you're finally going to settle down. When do I get to meet her?" "She is here probably getting ready. This is her ranch." "nice ranch." Mamie told Bear, "You had better go get ready. You don't want to miss your own wedding." "Not a chance Mamie." They all laughed. "Mamie there is someone I'd like you to meet before I go to get ready. It is a surprise for Sam." "Ok."

He lead her out to the stand where the music was all set up. Mamie took a deep breath. "It's my favorite Hawaiian singer...is it really him Bear?" Yes it is in the flesh." "Wow I sure do love your music." Dan says my music sure fits in with your wedding theme."

"Don't tell Sam that he is here." "Ok, now go and get dressed." Bear went to put on his Tuxedo and finished getting dressed. The sun was beginning to set. The lighting was perfect.

The Emerald Ring

Everybody was getting in place. It was about time to start. George was waiting for Bear to signal him to start singing. The usher lead Mamie and Rosemary to their seats. Donna started down the isle, next Debbie and her maid of honor Bobbie. They were all in place and now it is time for Sam. Uncle Don and Sam started down the isle. Bear nodded his head at George again and George started singing I Cross My Heart as she walked down the isle. Uncle Don handed Bear Sam's hand and they walked up the three steps leading to the altar to the Pastor . Behind the Pastor were three beautiful white columns with white sheers flowing in the breeze. There were two Grecian statues on each side. Everyone was waiting with anticipation for them to say I do. Finally the moment arrived and Bear and Sam said their vows. The Pastor announced them as husband and wife. "Ladies and Gentleman I'd like to introduce you to Mr. and Mrs. Jackson McBaine." Everyone stood up while they began to walk down the isle as husband and wife.

Bubbles start blowing all the way down the isle. Dan started singing an old song called Tiny Bubbles. Sam started laughing, "I can't believe you did that. How in the world did you get famous Dan to come to our wedding? Mamie loves him." "I know. Mamie has already

met him. Would you like to meet him?" "Yes."
"Come on."

"That sounded like George playing music
when I walked down the isle Tell me that wasn't
him." "Of course it was." "What miracle did you
perform to get him to come here?" "His whole
family is here." "I think I'm going to die." Bear
said, "Don't you dare!" "Sam I'd like to
introduce you to George." Sam said, "I love
your songs. You are the best." "I guess you
know you married a pretty special guy there." "I
knew that but I'm beginning to find out little by
little just how special he is."

"Dan come over here I want you to meet
my wife Sam." "Hi Dan. I'm so glad you're here.
You helped make our wedding very special and
I can't thank you enough. I just love you to
pieces for doing that." Bear says, "Wait a
minute now."

Everyone got in line to eat. After everyone
got their food and sat down at their table
Shamrock made a toast to Sam and Bear.
Gerry took all the pictures they wanted of their
wedding. Gerry told them that he will have their
wedding pictures all ready when they get back
from their honeymoon.

Sam got ready to throw her wedding

flowers. All the single women lined up. Sam threw her bouquet and Bobbie caught it. Sam looked at her and winked. Bear and Sam took off in their limo for their honeymoon. Everybody enjoyed the rest of the evening. Dusty and Tara danced the night away and spent the rest of the evening getting to know each other.

Sam and Bear are on their way to another great adventure.

Janet McBaine

About The Author

My name is Janet McBaine. I grew up in a very small town, Crossville Illinois, at the time my name was Janet Axe. I finished my last two years of high school in Columbia, Illinois.

My childhood was mostly spent going to school or during summer break fishing along the Wabash river or at the Blue Hole. I had lots of adventures growing up. My four brothers and I lived most of the time in the country. Lots of time to go exploring and live in a make believe world. That is where I learned to let my imagination soar. We didn't have all the high tech capabilities to tap into, we had to rely on our creative talents. Growing up I still hung onto my imagination and the ability to be creative and turn my hardships into adventures. God anointed me with the gift of writing at age 40. I have now finished two poem books, "Just for You" and "Collective Thoughts by Janet McBaine". I have two sequels planned for the Emerald Ring, "Underground P.A.' and "Missing in Superstition Mountain". A childrens book called Friends.

Summary

The book takes off setting up the story and

The Emerald Ring

leads you into a high intensity life story that won't let you put the book down. You never know what is going to happen next and can't wait to find out.

The story is about a young woman who has two men in love with her. One a very attractive corporate executive who owns the corporation she is trying to shut down. The woman's name is Samantha, Sam for short. Sam was raised by her grandfather after her parents were killed. He hired a housekeeper to care for Sam and to take care of the house for him. When her grandfather had passed on he left Sam with a lot of money and the ranch so she would be well taken care of.

Sam will take you into her bedroom where she has a hidden room behind a wall where she has her computer set up and where she practices martial arts. Lots of suprises are in store for you as you will meet lots of interesting characters as you go from one dilemma to another.

Sam will find herself in a high pursuit chase with Bear, the private detective when the bad guys find out that they have the evidence that will put them away for a long time. Sterling, the corporate owner, returns home to find out that his company has caught on fire, and that Sam is in a coma.

Will Sam come out of her coma? If she does, who will she choose, the good looking corporate executive or Bear the private detective who is quite the hunk. Some of you will want Sam to pick Sterling and some of you will be cheering for Bear. At the end you find again another twist to the story that will keep your mind wondering until the next sequel.

Are you ready to go on an incredibly journey? Let's go.

Now snuggle into your favorite chair and get you a cup of your favorite tea, coffee, or soft drink. Ready! Let's begin

The Emerald Ring

My husband Jackson E. McBaine (Bear) died
June 10,2004.
As I released him God received him and my
memory of him will live on throughout eternity.

18924266R00154

Made in the USA
San Bernardino, CA
04 February 2015